D1236150

PACIFIC AGONY

SEMIOTEXT(E) NATIVE AGENTS SERIES

Published by Semiotext(e)
2007 Wilshire Blvd., Suite 427, Los Angeles, CA 90057
www.semiotexte.com

The author sincerely thanks Matthew Stadler, Rich Jensen, and Clear Cut Press for their ingenuity in facilitating the experiences that led to writing this book.

Special thanks to Erik Morse.

Cover Photography by Scott Neary
Design by Hedi El Kholti

ISBN: 978-1-58435-082-8
Distributed by The MIT Press, Cambridge, Mass. and London, England
Printed in the United States of America

PACIFIC AGONY

a novel

Bruce Benderson

"To me, it seems a dreadful indignity to have a soul controlled by geography."

— George Santayana

My Dear Pacific Northwest Hosts,

…Why do they call it the Rim, a strangely smooth, liminal word for a brutal and terrifying cleavage? Rain is lashing the jagged coastline, and dark, wheeling birds are screeching. They travel in hordes, like locusts, over the few shrubs by the side of the highway, which strain against the merciless wind like shredded sails. Along the shore, the gnashing waves recoil from slippery rocks as if snarling. Who called these heaving seas "Pacific?"

Floating and crashing against each other in the water are the mammoth, decapitated trees whose branches were hacked off by collision; others are strewn along the beach, like the slimy, amputated limbs of shipwrecked giants. The logs lurch toward me, hitting the barrier of rocks, springing into the air like corks and landing back in the water in an explosion of spray. And through it all roils that sinister, vengeful fog.

Everything I've written has been wrong. With the hope of someday correcting this extended mistake, I'll hitchhike back to Port Angeles, put the attached into a mailbox…

Maybe you'll find some way to forgive this journey into error, because at last and too late it has pointed to a deeper awareness. Allow me, if you have the patience, to start at the beginning.

Impressions of the Pacific Northwest

by Reginald Fortiphton

~

Annotated by Narcissa Whitman Applegate of the
Willamette-Columbia Historical Legion and the
Daughters of the Oregon Trail Historical Committee

I

Turbulence

Times were cruel and full of mean spirits. Little by little, I'd been watching the rug pulled out from under my feet. For several years now, life had gone on in a surreal, viscous medium, transparent gelatin that stretched in response to gestures and condom-shrouded anything that wasn't flat. Even outrageous acting out no longer got any response.

Like a blackhead no one had bothered to pop, I kept a low profile on the smooth skin of this blandness. It was all the more insidious because of its flexibility. A strange new etiquette was grow-ing like an ameba, magically absorbing and denaturing the visceral.

My plane dove, swerved and rocked crazily from side to side; a child shrieked. I was pitched forward, and the seatbelt dug into my skin; but I barely noticed it because of that state of spleen holding me in a death grip, as we lurched across the continent from east to west. I was traveling in my most hated of the four seasons—fall—on the way to the kind of assignment that had taken on a feeling of bile but was being touted as an adventure. A small, fledging publishing cooperative had the unrealistic aim of enlivening Pacific Northwest culture and simultaneously giving the finger to the hegemonic world of New York media. So they'd invited me West to research a book on their region "seen through the eyes of a New Yorker." Supposedly, my perks were ready and waiting, including the broken-down roadster of the company's editor, a modest budget for food and gas, reservations at some funky lodgings and an idiosyncratic itinerary, all designed to procure me a kaleidoscopic platter of epiphanies and sound bytes.

A series of rapid shocks traveled through the body of the plane, like a convulsion. It set my pull-out tray vibrating, sloshing the vodka from edge to edge of the glass. This recalled to mind the precarious, perhaps uncontrollable situation I'd created for myself. How careful I'd been, in every e-mail and phone conversation, not to reveal my ruse. My eager hosts knew me as an urban essayist of some notoriety, a contemporary, though small-time, Tocqueville. From the quirky writing I'd forwarded in chapbooks and small volumes, they'd naively decided I was the perfect choice to produce a fresh take on their little corner of the world. It hadn't occurred to them that no successful writer would have jumped at such a poor deal, and they hadn't the slightest inkling that I was no "New York writer," either. Nor was I a real journalist, adventurer or travel writer—these were illusions I'd been prolonging with the smoke-and-mirror machinations of digital communication, by pretended e-mails from France or Eastern Europe or Southeast Asia. The truth was, this was the first trip I'd taken in over four years.

No, I hadn't gone anywhere since I'd left New York, after several embroilments scandalizing my upright family and putting my ankle in a homing bracelet, carefully monitored by the Justice Department for the last eighteen months. As soon as I was sentenced, I'd had no choice but to crawl back to my small, depressed *ville natale* in upstate New York and move into the basement of our family home, which was still occupied by my ancient, hideously intrusive mother.

This fresh reentry into the world might explain in part the hypersensitivity I felt in regard to every detail around me. I was like a man confined to a cave who finds himself horribly blinded when he first emerges into the light. What's more, the monitoring bracelet had come off just a week ago, and the irritation it had caused around my ankle prolonged that prickly sensation of confinement and censure; the spot still felt annoyingly sore. I bent down to rub it as the plane suddenly jerked forward, slamming the top of my head against the seat in front.

A bruise was just the thing I didn't need at this juncture—or any sign of disfigurement suggesting a dangerous lifestyle and causing my hosts to do further research on my whereabouts for the last several months. So I pressed an ice cube from the glass of vodka to the pain, to squeeze out the swelling.

At any rate, I wasn't too optimistic about this assignment. During my high-rolling years as a peripatetic journalist, I'd already been sent to the Pacific Northwest on assignment; and true to my Huysmansesque suspicions of modernity, I had long ago formulated an albeit racist hypothesis about its allegedly progressive people. The Northwest—Seattle, Portland, Eugene, etc.—all the stops on the itinerary, were, I accused, "New England pretending to be California." California was, in my mind, already a pretense, and I expected to find the chilly populace of this region even more cheerfully hypocritical.

I gazed out my window on the sea of dark clouds as my shaking seat jiggled the image into double vision; and I pictured the flat, geometrically divided western landscapes below, wondering why anyone still bothered to travel in this cookie-cutter country. What was the use of visiting identical reproductions of the same Wal-Mart or adding new encounters of equally streamlined mentality to the roster? As far as I was concerned, everything was a part of the same fabric, woven for years in the drab bungalows of suburban North America.

Of course, I'd concealed all these judgments from my hosts, who'd absolutely no idea when they invited me of the prejudices under which I labored. They didn't know that I saw their region—which the guidebooks revealed as 87% Caucasian—as little more than one more smug gated community, abysmally unaware of its own identity, disguising its grudging repression as laid-backness and equality, its proper politeness as something mellow.[1]

Moreover, I had little use for what I deemed their pithless speech, excised as it was of colorful opinions or pointed references to ethnicity. Why wouldn't they understand that, under a guise of inclusiveness, they'd erased all the sharp particularities of cultural types? In the reedy tones of the missionary, they proclaimed their absence of prejudice; but this was only because they'd subjected diversity to a draconian homogenization. Among their Jews there seemed to be a deplorable lack of irony; their Catholics had lost most of the gutsy emotionality prevalent in the southern countries of their origins. The studied politeness of their Asians seemed indistinguishable to me from their own squeaky-clean, WASP-derived insipidness. To tame those

---

1. As counterpoint to this obviously skewed viewpoint, I urge you to take note of a more balanced perspective in some of our popular contemporary guides to the region, as, for example: [sic] "There's something quirky to life up in the left-hand corner of the USA and southwest Canada... This is a culture founded on *restless idealism*, and there is the strong, slightly uneasy sense that there's still more exploring to do. The Northwest is a long way from the traditional centers of mainstream culture and power, *and the locals like it that way!*" [italics and punctuation mine]—Lonely Planet's *Pacific Northwest*.

underclass members of the Latino population, on the other hand, they'd crafted a pejorative vocabulary that condemned boisterous behavior in the name of order and community, without discussing any of this in the context of ethnic identity, and while primly silencing anybody who did with hokey charges of "racial profiling." The people of this region (and by *people* I meant middle-class people, for only they had the power to set the tone) were a tight-knit hegemonic enclave, who'd exterminated any words that could describe their particularities and thereby threaten their unspoken ascendancy.[2] Aside from that, all I could imagine were a smattering of demoralized youth, self-styled anarchists who wiled the time away playing State of Emergency[3] or listening to obscure bands I'd never heard of like The Fartz.[4]

---

2. A cliché response common of quite a few newcomers. Elaborate types try to mystify it, but the simple truth is, we know that by letting others think we're a little stodgy and not that accessible, we're simply keeping it secret that we live in one of the most beautiful parts of the nation.

3. A Sony PlayStation 2 game about an urban riot, set in the near future in which a fantasized American Trade Organization, known as the ATO, has declared a state of emergency, filling the streets with officers in riot gear. The player's objective is to attack and crush as many officers as possible. Destruction of property and attacks on innocent bystanders are allowed. See www.absolute-playstation.com for more information.

4. One of Seattle's earliest hardcore punk groups, known to attack what they considered governmental and religious corruption, racism, sexism, poverty. According to my research, in 1998 Jello Biafra's Alternative Tentacles label put out a retrospective album of the group entitled *Because This Fuckin' World Still Stinks*. I seem to be "hipper" than thou, Fortiphton, or maybe I'm a less lazy researcher.

My musings were producing an unpleasant sensation of constriction in my neck and soldiers. I wriggled grotesquely until a passing flight attendant to whom I'd already taken a passionate dislike faked an idiotic, comforting smile above two chins, which branded my sensibilities like a hot poker on bare flesh—because I knew what it meant: "So glad you're practicing some of the in-seat stretching exercises we recommended."

I wanted to tell her that the tension coiling through my body wasn't fueled by sitting in one place, but only by her own cloying, hypocritical smile, as well as by the inane announcements that her male counterpart was making through the speakers: a schlocky hie-dee-ho to those passengers who'd been stupid enough to agree that it was their birthday, followed by a hokey comic routine about a supposedly lost Rolex and an intention to appropriate it, which won a few nervous laughs.

There was, in fact, something unbearably grotesque about these attempts at casual humor in the face of the militaristic body checks we'd all endured as we passed through the metal detector and they confiscated my only possession of value, my much beloved eighty-dollar Dupont lighter. And I suppose it was the flatulent pulsing of these thoughts in my head that made me, as if in a dream, take a permanent marker from my bag and draw a fat *X* across the liquid crystal screen in the seat in front of me, currently showing a segment from the *Style* channel. Then, as usual, anxiety spiked through me at the possibility of being nabbed by the loathsome attendant with the idiotic smile; and I sullenly draped my jacket over the screen to cover my crime.[5]

---

5. Apparently presented as a light-hearted prank, but vandalism is no minor infraction. Our own region can't claim to be free of it, and currently it occurs

Par for the course. In my case, a sense of culpability about one thing always foreshadows punishment by the things that are to follow. An unbearable foreboding passed over me as I thought of the hospitality I'd accepted from my Northwest publishing host, a Caucasian gay man who'd fathered a child with a lesbian. Would I, I wondered, be subjected to the nauseating odors and saccharine endearments of their domesticity? And if so, would I be able to conceal my cranky cynicism in the face of their well-meant hospitality?

Surreptitiously, I dipped my napkin several times into the cup of vodka on the pull-out tray and, like an old lady who has spilled soup on her sensible skirt, began rubbing furiously at the bold X I'd made over the liquid crystal screen in my fit of gall. It had, of course, little effect upon the now dry permanent ink. With frustration I dumped the rest of the vodka—blackened by the ink—onto the floor and smashed the cup under my foot. Then I wrapped it in the sodden napkin and stowed both in the pocket under the pullout tray. No syrupy flight attendant stooping to collect refuse would be given the chance to notice my infraction, if I had anything to say about it. What rash surge of rebelliousness had made me think I was capable of dealing with a confrontation as I whipped out my poison magic marker?

In this atmosphere of total alienation, jostled by the turbulence, I settled into that acute and unpleasant sense of my own

---

at both ends of the political spectrum. The Animal Liberation Front has taken credit for a number of these crimes in Oregon, including a 1991 fire at a plant that made food for mink farms, not to mention criminal defacement of the Washington State University animal-testing laboratories. Regardless of which side you're on, this is no joke!

body. It was as if the postmodern present into which I'd been dumped had taken everything away from me but its reality. During my time of amorous copulation with street people in New York (another story), I'd enjoyed the poor's heavy emphasis on the body as their inalienable source of strength and identity.[6] The thought was of little comfort to me now, because I could sense my own body's slow deterioration, knew that I was at the beginning of an irreversible physical decline. Suffice it to say at this point that my bitterness and sense of disenfranchisement had once blithely impelled me through life's shadows and expressed themselves in lusty, libidinous rebellion; but now, waning energy was making this same alienation just about intolerable.

Happily, as the Gorgon of a flight attendant teetered past me for a last check to make sure that seats were upright and belongings stowed, she magically avoided looking my way; and moments later, with eyes squeezed tight, I felt the plane ineptly bouncing along the ground to the tune of gasping breaths and the to-be-expected shrieking of the overly pampered child behind me. I stood unsteadily on my swollen legs, ripped my belongings from the compartment above and shoved my way through the crowd.

The blond and affable, slightly corpulent young man waiting for me at the airport was a Western entrepreneur of sorts, with a

---

6. Or, as put in writing by Mr. Fortiphton, in an unpublished text later found in his papers, "[The poor] were like vital, valuable goods [sic] that had been mishandled… and their statuesque brutality, liquid eyes, and exhibitionistic stances intrigued me more than the carefully conditioned and cleaned bodies of my own class." Perhaps author is lacking in the fifth—or olfactory—sense.

business connection I barely understood to the defunct Nirvana, a band whose vague mythology of pseudo-rebellion I judged as flirting ineptly with a working-class ethos and touting a tepid suburban existentialism. He was now responsible for the financial backing of the publishing company—in fact, I think the money for my trip had come directly from him—and had volunteered in that feisty Far-West, lend-a-hand-way to chauffeur me to the hotel they'd booked for me. His perky, relentless chatter was peppered with socio-historical allusions to what he referred to as the Pacific Rim, which clued me into the fact that he was expecting the book I would write for him to contain observations and insights of a similar tenor.

A dark cloud of malicious pleasure engulfed me as I thought of all the ways I was about to disappoint his bushy-tailed expectations, but his chatter continued to pelt me with cleverisms, while all I could think was how goddam much I needed a smoke.

I was, unfortunately, ancient enough to recall a time of smoking sections in planes—exotic and devil-may-care as it now seems—when "stews,"[7] all under thirty, I might add, in fetchingly majorette-style outfits, fawned over you with the question, "Coffee, tea, or milk?" This isn't to say that I was ever a connoisseur of female flesh, I had merely enjoyed the campy spectacle. Nowadays the loss of both—the right to smoke as well as the right to be surrounded by a swarm of young, doting unliberated Tinkerbells who'd been chosen for their attention and measurements rather than their aviation skills (brought home by the quaint offer of "milk," a menu item itself

---

7. Stewardesses, the archaic term for flight attendant.

poignantly reminiscent of the innocent past)—only increased my black despair.

I assumed I needn't even ask permission to smoke in my host's car. It would, on the improbable chance that should he not object, lower the resale value, for god's sake. So without any explanation and with, perhaps, a touch of hostility, I let my luggage crash to the concrete and quite impudently lit up, after which my first exhale quite accidentally, but in my eyes, rather fortuitously, enveloped the mini-knapsacked child who'd screamed behind me during landing.

To my astonishment, my host seemed absolutely indulgent about my archaic peccadillo, and as I took large drags from the cigarette into damaged lungs convulsed with coughs, he merely stole the opportunity to pepper my ears with more pell-mell sociological observations. Later in the car, he was equally as gracious and unperturbed by the clouds of smoke coming from my orifice.

He was a graduate of the grunge years of Seattle counterculture and, aside from being no critic of smokers, took pride in his pithy deconstruction of all his city's neo-mercantile prohibitions. His was a more articulate and original version of the type of discourse I'd encountered from his generation, which had replaced, I surmised, the more sensationalistic bohemian poses of my youth with a kind of bemused anti-capitalist cynicism.[8] However, I soon lost the thread of his arguments, preferring

---

8. In an email dated August 17, in a kind of aside, the author finally responded to my multiple requests for his age. He claimed that experience had taught him the wisdom of never revealing it publicly, but that he fell within the category of "dirty old man," current usage of which would seem to refer to an individual over forty-eight.

instead to let my eyes run over his milk-fed skin, hardy Alpine features (I'd soon find the look prevalent here), rather husky frame and urban-ironic clothes (a brown hound's-tooth overcoat, circa 1960), worn, I surmised, to evoke a kind of postmodern sophistication yet suggestive, in ways I suspected he could be unaware, of entitled bourgeois academia.

No matter, for my degenerate libido was already sizing him up for an exploitation in the form of a sociopathic toss in the hay (a "one-night affair, baby"[9]), although I was impudently aware that he was not only heterosexual but married, which, as far as I was concerned, added sauce to my potential amorous aggression. I was certainly no respecter of marriage, nor of any faithful dyad for that matter, and many times in the past had ended up preying on a still youthful hubby partly for the pleasure of shaking up his domestic tranquility. There was always a way, though it sometimes necessitated a "dosing."

At any rate and truth be told, this impulse now arose in me more from a demeaning neediness, a pitiful lack, than from any penchant for political activism based on my critique of the nuclear family. Rather than dampening my hunger for the flesh of other humans, social alienation and waning energy, to my increasing dismay, at this rather advanced age, had only succeeded in aggravating my libido.

My companion couldn't have seemed more blithely unaware of these base thoughts running through my head. On and on he chirped, building a protective shield of expectations of me as a pithy social critic with a leftist orientation between himself and the dark, resentful cipher I actually was. He was

9. From Esther Phillips, "One Night Affair" 1972(?).

driving me, before even stopping at the hotel, through rain—which would follow me throughout this journey like a constant rebuke—to a site he seemed certain of clinching our imaginary political copulation: a tiny park on Diagonal Avenue South, inserted between a federal government warehouse, shipping containers and other industrial structures on the bank of the Duwamish River.[10]

The park had been established in the 1980s in what I deemed a laughable fit of civic mea culpa to alert visitors to the tragic history of the spot: a series of greedy land seizures, beginning with diversions of the river in 1905 to make room for industry, which had transformed it from the home of a supposedly utopian aboriginal community of Indians, who had lived uninterrupted off the river's fauna since the sixteenth century, into a highly profitable wharf. The process, neatly outlined on two self-accusing billboards, had been particularly messy, since the original natives had inconveniently stuck around in houseboats parked near the white settlers long enough to die of starvation in the 1920s, when the river had become little more than a flow of noxious chemicals, and the megalomaniac plans of the fledgling white industrialists had begun to pick up steam (so to speak). Now all that remained of the presence of either Indian or early white settler on this perhaps most polluted river on the continent was this rather skanky, cramped urban park, its view of the Trans-America pyramid and its benches of plastic (recycled, they were proud to point out), near which my young host was currently standing on his metaphorical soapbox.

---

10. Official government status: Public Access Shoreline, est. 1986.

Eerily, he seemed to find the ruthless injustice of the macabre transformation and these unstoppable industrialists a dark topic to savor, and at one point even betrayed a giddy admiration for their ceaselessly monotone ambition, which he gleefully suggested would even have allowed them "to pioneer Mars!"

"Looks like a concentration camp," I observed.

"There *was* no utopic period," he countered, in a joust for the most cynical. "Seattle has been totally remade from the beginning."

His narrative was, to my ears, typical of contemporary hip mentality in its recent incarnation as decadent social critic. Apparently, the Emperor Neroes of our new intelligentsia were watching the mown path of modernity with wry eyes and inviting their acolytes (me, in this case) to partake of this sick spectacle from a choice seat in the virtual theater (or should I say stadium): noble savages gulped by the yawning maws of all-devouring global capitalism, as we, the bemused yet paralyzed meta-critics, clucked. But his discourse, which was even rather rigorous, wasn't the cause of the bile leaking through me at this particular moment, in thicker flux than the poisons to be found in the river. It was the discovery of the other guests who shared this sliver of public space with the container ships.

Fucking artists!

It seems the port of Seattle had deemed it moral to dot this site of past slaughter with generously spacious lofts for this new flock of doomed squatters—producers, no doubt, of the usual flaccid conceptualist gestures, political tinkerers and *bricoleurs* at best.

After seeing the ruthless renovation by artist-homesteaders of other, once humble neighborhoods, I'd come to view these spineless double agents—artists—as nothing more than the front guard and first wave of bourgeois gentrification. Patsies all of global capitalism's tidal wave, contemporary artists had recently been demoted in my mind to the lowest rung of collaborators with the powers that be, unconsciously bringing their incipient middle-class values with smug righteousness into poor neighborhoods—and later gloating with mock surprise at their skyrocketing property values, soon upheld, of course, by their dour block associations and neighborhood watches with a distinctly racist cast, which succeeded, inevitably, in shooing libido and energy from their street corners.

By now we were finally heading for the hotel, and at the thought of it new fears constricted my already strangulated throat, making the stiff smiles with which I was attempting to greet the clever conversation of my young chauffeur less and less easy to execute. On the phone I'd been adamant about my absolute inability to endure hotel chains, citing as reasons their careful segregation of smokers from the rest of the population, their fruity room deodorizers that were an insult to nature and probably more carcinogenic than tobacco smoke, and their glass-wrapped-in-paper pretensions of cleanliness, when it absolutely had to be the case that someone at some point before you had done something unspeakable on the polyester bedspread on which you were currently lolling.

My hosts had claimed to understand my reservations and had quite gallantly assured me that I would not be subjected to such "touristic" phenomena. But this did not, by any means, allay a sudden apprehension, presently coating my esophagus with a gagging feeling as if someone had forced one of the aforementioned deodorizers (Wildflower Bouquet, let us assume) between my struggling lips and pushed the button. Even more insidious, in my opinion, than hotel chains, were those proverbial "guest houses" designed for the same middling classes, vulgar facsimiles of historical authenticity that were usually accented by some cloying pastoral element—a bed canopy or a porcelain pitcher. They always stridently demanded a strict code of respectability that made you end up walking around on tiptoe.

I'd already been subjected to one such Disneyed environment in the Pacific Northwest several years ago when the well-meaning organizer of a woman's book discussion group, for a reading she had most generously organized on my behalf to promote one of my travel books, had briefly housed me on Capitol Hill—Seattle's ghetto for individuals of homosexual persuasion—in a quaint Victorian guesthouse held by a gentrifying leather queen. This had immediately caused some embarrassing tension between me and my sponsor. To her perplexity, I'd bitterly protested my spotlessly clean room and its placid view of a manicured garden, its white chenille bedspread, its tastefully arranged antiques of a decidedly masculine cast and many subtly placed notes on linen stationary enjoining guests to behave as if they were in their own home (whatever that meant), while keeping an eye toward water conservation and reigning one's sexual exploits to a low decibel.

Of course, the kinds of lodging I could tolerate were now scarce as hen's teeth (to keep up the pastoral idioms). They'd existed in every city of every size in the fairly recent past and could be identified by the presence of terminal guests who paid by the month—refugees from the world of family values, dubbed "bachelors" or "spinsters" in their day—as well as other single-income singles, including impoverished retirees, widowers and denizens of the many forms of urban petty crime. All of these people had been seeking the cacophonous solace of city life in a site now rendered anachronistic by mall culture but formerly called "downtown," which had offered conveniently located places of nourishment for the kitchenless single, dry cleaners and the like, without requiring the use of an automobile. This downtown, in a word, had been a place that obliged tourists and permanent residents to share the same environment, thereby granting the tourist himself a more realistic urban experience. I wanted, to put it simply, a "bachelor hotel."

Certainly my older readers will be struck by a glimmer of recognition in hearing this term for an authentic habitation, rapidly being extinguished by suburban raids into urban terrain that bring with them their glum insistence upon child-friendly streets, piped-in TV entertainment and ugly structures meant to house their SUV's. But I knew there was only a minuscule chance of getting what I wanted.

As we sped toward this final reckoning, I forced myself out of professional duty to look through the window at the wet, slippery gradients of the pretentiously Victorian Queen Anne Hill on my left; and a cold chill traveled up and down my spine as I wondered if this was where I would be deposited. It was already dark, and rain slathered the windows, producing a visual distortion I welcomed, since any distortion at all of what usually met my eyes provided some relief to me.

We were passing, my host gallantly indicated, Pioneer Square, that smidgen of old Seattle, which conjured a fantasy image of the former city before the great fire of 1889, based on my reading. It had originally been a mishmash of log cabins and lumber mills and was not even a boomtown until 1897, when a ship nearly sinking under the weight of two tons of gold brought in from the Yukon anchored in its port, an event that soon drew thousands of new speculators stopping off to stock up on their way north.

However, the city I liked to imagine existed even before this notoriety. Bizarrely, it had been built along boardwalks on First Avenue, all of them balanced precariously on stilts, barely holding human life out of the lapping sea's reach as it roiled constantly around ankles, threatening the permanence of the place.

In those days, apparently, few streets could be distinguished from the sea itself at high tide; and loggers, storekeepers and whores alike waded through the quagmire, eking out watery survival like determined, mud-streaked beavers. Yesler Way, in fact, which still skirts the southern boundary of Pioneer Square, wasn't at all pedestrian friendly: logs skidded down it on their way to Henry Yesler's mill on the pier, winning it the moniker "Skid Road," a term that soon came to designate other degenerate urban spaces all over the country.

It was not water, curiously, that swallowed this first and muddy incarnation of the city; it was fire, which inhaled boardwalk and building like Godzilla its rollercoaster.[11] The new city that rapidly took shape, built by the obstinate hands of those tenacious settlers whom my young host had already described as

---

11. Another cryptic, and probably poorly researched, allusion. *Godzilla*, 1959, apparently, the first and most terrible, who destroyed a wooden roller coaster as if it were made of toothpicks.

being capable of "pioneering Mars," became a permanent monument to the overweening appetite of Modernity, in whose late-stage jaws I now felt myself writhing. Brick, steel and stone replaced the whimsical wooden structures; inlets were filled in; and the new city, whose foundations were four feet higher than the previous, literally buried the old that had communed so quaintly with the sea, confining that past to an underground morgue of catacombs.

Just a year after the Great Fire of 1890, our worthy Seattle survivalists revealed their brand of multiculturism by crowning triangular Pioneer Square with a totem pole stolen from the Tlingit Indians. When it, too, was burned, the allegedly more enlightened and diplomatic city fathers, still feeling sentimental about their roots, graciously offered the Tlingit a handsome wage to carve another. The Indians, who were quickly acquiring the manipulative skills of good capitalists, accepted the offer and money with a dignified handshake, then sat on it indefinitely, until a second payment was made for the new carving.

As for the handsome pergola in Pioneer Square, it was merely a ladylike attempt to hide a public lavatory. Quickly I scrawled a note to myself: "quagmire, logs, gold, greed, theft, shit, fire." Such, it seems, were at the foundations of the city's civic pride.

We were headed, I was suddenly informed to my relief, not to a quaint renovated Victorian mansion, but to the nearby International District, a mostly Asian quarter centered around Fifth and Seventh avenues and Weller and Jackson streets. My hotel was the dapper yet funky Panama, lost by its Japanese owners during the internment. And it turned out to be, to my great relief, a single-occupancy residence worthy of any *flâneur*.

Temporarily ignoring the authentic-to-the-letter new teahouse, placidly glowing in welcoming earth tones through a window on the ground floor, I passed under the reassuringly garish neon sign and up the worn but well-swept stairs. Seattle may have coagulated in my mind as a squeaky-clean dormitory for fledgling dot-com-ers,[12] I told myself with the first sigh of relief since I'd climbed in emotional disarray from the plane, but here finally was an environment that wouldn't compromise the abject cynicism of a weary urban theorist, whom too many insisted on dubbing a crank.

Even the room itself, though clean as a whistle, reflected a suitably Hopperesque desolation: an iron bedstead circa 1950, cheap flowered bedspread, despondently brown wooden paneling perfect for meditating and old TV with askew aerial. There was a sober masculine quality to the room and something—may I say—"Oriental" about it. Through the window I could see a shadowy street corner swept by oblique daggers of rain, through which I could spot a shuttered establishment of doubtful reputability, embellished by a sign of a cartoonish cocktail glass. Then a chance to drown the formulaic drone of media-saturated middle America in alcohol actually was still being offered to some rejected souls in need of comfort?

Most iconic of all, however, was my little white sink in place of a personal bathroom, more evocative of Modernism's *machine célibataire* than the most precious Surrealist *objet*—used to pee,

---

12. Hee hee. Pardon my astonished amusement, because misinformation is never a case for laughter. But how could the author fail to be aware that Seattle was, and is more and more, an *international center* of high-tech industry, the home of Boeing and Microsoft, to name a few.

most probably, by countless former numbers of the night's disentranced and unmoored, too drunk or too exhausted by labor to stumble to the lavatory in the hall.

Almost cheerfully, I unpacked my few clothes and copious pharmaceuticals—acid-reducers, migraine tablets, laxatives, stool softeners and a couple of emergency personal enemas, as well as a heart medicine used to relieve urination problems caused by an enlarged prostate (for how long now had I been suffering the myriad symptoms of modern stress!)—and fell onto the creaky bed so that I could resume my reading of *Là-bas*;[13] but something, as usual, was wrong. It was freezing in here![14]

Then came a new foreboding, which had somehow been pushed to the recesses of my subconscious: it was likely to rain tomorrow and the day after, and the day after that. For me, the sun and its heat were far more than a pretext for simple cheerfulness or an afternoon of recreation. Their absence was yet another crushing symbol of a hijacked culture. But what could I do? Spreading my jacket over the bedspread, I settled down to try to sleep in room 362.[15]

----

13. The Satanic novel (1884) of J.-K. Huysmans, often accused of severe degeneracy.

14. Most accredited Seattle hotel rooms registered with the Bureau of Lodgings and Hotels are kept at a comfortable 65-68 degrees. However, numerous recent studies readily available to the general public link heavy smoking to poor circulation and lowered body temperature. Look inward for once, Fortiphton.

15. Why does author present the room number? It adds absolutely no relevant information to this text and, if any of the room details are wrong (which I can't check), leaves him open to charges of misinformation.

II

The Sun in Calumny

*"Sure am glad somebody found
something to do with 'em."*

The next morning, waking with the flowered quilt pulled to my
shoulders against the chill, as though rudely surprised in disha-
bille, and thinking of the rain-soaked existence of the locals, I
wondered if I were the last person to remember the supremacy
of the Sun, the fact that it was the nerve center of Antiquity's
spiritual and religious life, its core, its clarity, its kernel; that
there was a time when a prime requirement for ascendancy was
living in a land where sunlight was plentiful. I wanted to throw
open the window and shout into the streets (although I feared
a blast of cold, wet air) that Greeks and Latins worshiped this
star and had contempt for the barbarians upon whom it sparsely
shone; that the Ancients' armor was polished to glitter blind-
ingly under it in battle; that they took pleasure in exercising
naked beneath its rays; and that their pomp, display and etiquette
(all sorely absent from the environment in which I now found
myself) were attempts to emulate its brilliance.

Now, in my opinion, the paradigm had shifted, and the
reins had been handed to the sunless places. I'd always found
morbid amusement in questioning people—with supposed
innocence—about their favorite season. Autumn was almost

universally the answer, and it was a season that seemed permanently ensconced in this region. Why not summer, I would wonder, with its indolent breezes and lush floral array, its bright petaled heads lifted in ignorance of the coming slaughter? Or at least, spring and its violent transformations, its days getting longer, its tyranny of green? But autumn? Yes, today most people preferred fall's morbid pageant, the slow, albeit colorful, funeral march toward winter's stasis, a progressive darkening of the heavens, trees stripped of their finery like Jesus of his garments, but most of all, those chilly breezes.

This emphasis on hardy freshness, I soon surmised, had to be based on certain cultural characteristics, for every civilization must find its likeness in the phenomena of Nature. The "autumn people" now in ascendance, then, were those of the North, like this place of rain and gloomy skies; and it was no accident that they should bring their penchant for coolness—in hiking boots, tartans and L. L. Bean paraphernalia—down upon our heads. In a world in which the North now controlled trade, language and culture, they were, obviously, Earth's new tyrants. The reign of the sun, the hegemony of the undressed and the tanned, had been over for centuries. Nature for these new tyrants was no warm, embracing mother, no golden body dappled by sunlight, nor the ring of gentle ripples left behind by a bronzed Narcissus, but something muffled and booted. They were the same people who, under the guise of saving energy, kept their thermostats at 60 degrees and wore several layers inside, finding even their own homes no place for skin to contact air.

It was astonishing to note the accuracy with which moral values marched in time to meteorological preferences, I'd always

thought; all the chilly virtues: independence and industrious-
ness, self-reliance, plain speech and the tight lip were the gods
of these sun-deprived people. Expansion, rhetoric, exaggera-
tion, interdependence within a benign hierarchy, sensuality,
ceremony, display, warmth (and here my ice-cold hand in this
barely heated room crept below the quilt)—all the qualities
that had brought the antique world its glory—found no welcome before the dull embers of the Northern hearth. For
several centuries now, the tribes of the North had triumphed
over the sun-drenched empires of old, and after stealing the
mantle of history, they had fitted it to their tastes. The power
of the Sun, currently defamed through discourses about skin
cancer and holes in the ozone layer, was being extinguished,
and with it, I maintained, that clear light that linked our intel-
lects to our senses.

Consequently, as I lit up a smoke, resentment for the patter
of rain outside my window and the hearty chill that filled my
hotel room, in mocking conjunction with the silence of the
nonworking steam radiator, merged in my mind with this
lauded of late industrious city. I conjured its people, cheerful
and chilly and clipped, in their cardigans and long underwear,
pushing through the silvery mists of its streets in search of anti-
septic mastery. Nonetheless, I did feel fortunate to have been
placed in a hotel managed by people of the Orient, who normally had no seasonal bias but adapted to the changing cycles
with the eclectic openness of true connoisseurs. They rearranged
their rooms to integrate their lives into Nature's kaleidoscope, to
view cherry blossoms in June, moonlight on snow in January.
They never padded their bodies too tightly against the elements
but always adapted to them.

The thought gave me the strength to rise and dress, after adding my own golden effluvium to that receptacle of historical bachelorhood mentioned earlier; and when I ventured into the hallway, seeing it in the light of day for the first time, I was impressed by its dowdy authenticity and once more thought of one cold season I had spent in Kyoto, when my quite loosely garbed landlady had hovered decorously around a charcoal stove.

Downstairs in the tearoom, I marveled at the genuine Japanese pottery lovingly displayed in a glass cabinet and studied the historical photographs of the formal, placid faces of former local Japanese businessmen and women. Before the internment, one of whom had kept an establishment dubbed "Hotel Hiroshima." The poignancy of the reference was probably what caused me to blurt conspiratorially to a softly smiling attendant with velvety, glazed eyes, who was on his way to make up a room, "Great place. Don't let them do some kind of horrible renovation." Concealing the fact that he understood the implication, he answered stonily, "Just cleaning."

As I emerged from the building, my niece Sophie and her husband Peewee greeted me exuberantly. They'd moved here almost twenty years ago from the East, and having heard I was in town, were excitedly anticipating showing me the sights.

Perhaps some explanation is due. It must be obvious by now that these words spill from a brain long ago convoluted by suffering, an aggressive power cell left too long to marinate in the acidic tear drops of self-pity; but to my relatives, and indeed, even to strangers, I often appear to be a mild, self-effacing mouse. In this modern age pulsing with stimuli, skills of perception may have so weakened that the sullen defeat leaking in torrents from my tired eyes and curling my lips into a rictus of disgust, or tinting my complexion with a pall, are, as a rule, overlooked by interlocutors, who often declare finding me "sweet." I've also been christened a number of times, usually by females, with the condescending appellation "adorable," in its meaning of something flaccidly likeable and squishy—ineffectual, in a word, a kind of Pillsbury doughboy. And indeed, these sobriquets are not far off the mark; for despite the vitriol coursing through my veins, I am, I suppose, a coward, who suppresses or barely mumbles the imprecations spiking through his witchlike spirit. It's true that my disgust had found an outlet once or twice in the heat of certain passionate, jealous attachments, such as the time I'd tried to smash the skull of a Times Square homeboy paramour against a subway turnstile. But those who were less intimate saw only tamed defeat, which they enjoyed labeling with impotent-sounding terms of endearment. And such were the perceptions of good old Sophie and Peewee, who took my often-laconic style as good old-fashioned shyness.

As was their wont, they'd taken me first to a threadbare notions store in what was left of the downtown area, as part of an affectionate makeover campaign. It was an old routine of Sophie's, making over Uncle Reggie; and this time, on her insistence, I clutched a just purchased shopping bag with a bottle of hair coloring labeled "Winsome Wheat," guaranteed, she assured me in a tone that threatened an upcoming chuck under the chin, to "lighten you up, Unc," as well as "bring the fillies running."

Peewee, whom I suspected abused her, was expounding on the benefits of aerobics and light weights for the transformation of my drooping gut into something called a "six-pack"—about as desirable, as far as I was concerned, as the couch-potato sound of that beery appellation. He was a small, tense, thick fireplug of a man, a criminal investigator for an insurance company who'd dragged my niece from an Eastern city to a suburb of Seattle called "Redmond," apparently so obscurely located that they'd had trouble finding my hotel.

"What kind of place is that you're staying?" mused Sophie with a wrinkled nose that pantomimed "yuk." "If you want I can drive in with some clean sheets."

I good-naturedly shrugged off the offer, protesting with a tad more vehemence when they began insisting on reinstalling me in their home, in a bedroom they'd built out of their second garage. "It's probably for the best," Sophie relented. "The rabbit traps we set around the garden would probably keep you up all night."

These remarks, however, reached me as if I were at the bottom of a well, because we were still standing in some part of Seattle's downtown, but not the part that has been transformed into a spruced-up showplace, a cavalcade of economic history; no, this was a forgotten once-important street—I don't even recall the name. And its few unrenovated buildings—especially a certain sad pharmacy with a dilapidated notions counter holding exhausted bottles of never purchased cologne, under harsh fluorescents and among faded cardboard displays, like leftover poems of a simpler time—were bringing back memories of a relatively idyllic childhood in my small urban locality in upstate New York, whose downtown was now nearly decimated.

During those mid-century years, my father, a businessman, worked in a Neogothic turn-of-the-century office building, and my visits to him there were brief but remembered with longing. In those days, "downtown" was a genuine social arena, a catch-all world of work and commerce where people often appeared unaccompanied by family members. These shopkeepers, lawyers, cleaning ladies, unmarried secretaries, cigarette-smoking drop-outs, truants, cripples, window washers, bachelor hair dressers, dentists, elevator operators, chiropractors, accountants, soda jerks, bellboys, construction workers, vagrants, alcoholics, divorced barmaids and probation officers ate in public places in front of one another, rather than in the bosom of any family. Astonishingly, they lived lives separate from the family circle.

There was, in addition, in my downtown, that old-fashioned local department store that was no part of a chain, which had a block-long series of windows with surreal shadow-box narratives involving mannequins, as well as a mechanism that sprayed samples of the latest perfume into the air for passersby (before the vogue for scent allergies[16]). The store's interior was redolent with the odor of freshly polished wooden display cabinets; and its inventory of stockings, gloves, ties, brassieres and other accoutrements was catalogued and arranged obsessively as if for the most demanding of fetishists. This store's uniformed elevator operators, highly made-up perfume counter clerks, gloves on

---

16. He is unaware, apparently, of the epidemic in allergies to contemporary scent ingredients, a problem taken very seriously by the governments of the Western states. For example, Evergreen College, one of our more progressive Washington State institutions, now expressly forbids the use of scent on campus and stipulates that any student wearing perfume or oils please leave the classroom.

plaster hands, illuminated women's lingerie cases, plaster torsos outfitted with girdles, and largely unmonitored dressing rooms promised vague, sometimes transgressive pleasures.

I remember our town's two or three great department stores because they were major loci of my fantasy world from the time I first visited one at four and a half years old, holding my mother's hand to buy an Eaton suit with a matching woolen cap. Aside from exposure to new odors and three-paneled mirrors, there was the strange, light touch of the tape-measure-wielding tailor and the presence of my mother in her cinch-waisted suit, standing nearby. But today, of course, such labor and consumption are organized in a more simplistic fashion. Shopping has lost the eroticism of saturating one special terrain; grim supply depots called malls and "outlets" have taken the place of these compressed fantasy landscapes. Military in their uniformity, shorn of either high-bourgeois sophistication or mom-and-pop familiarity, these new places assault the eye with their insipid brightness. Transportation to and from them is confined to individual family vehicles; travel by foot is left to the few who are both underage and unsupervised, or to the destitute, public transportation being only for the handicapped or elderly.

But somewhere in my memory, like a field in a clearing, the vast spaces of these stores survive, as does my father's office building, with its polished terrazzo floors, echoing marble lobby, candy-and-cigarette counter and orange-lit hallways; all of which have, needless to say, been replaced by a suburban office complex with an anonymous car port.

Such were the poetic ideas coursing through me in this still unregenerate downtown venue of contemporary Seattle, as I watched the few disabled or homeless straggle by and Sophie and Peewee's shuffling impatience began to fade out. I remembered how downtown had been a seedy landscape for many of my first libidinal shenanigans (in the bus station, the library lavatory, the sculpture garden of the museum, the locker room, the hotel lobby, the fitting room and the downtown street corner); and I wondered if an older Seattle had once concealed the same secret pleasures.

Sophie saw the pang of longing on my face and took my hand, leading me to the monorail, which deposited us at the Experience Music Project, an ungrammatically hybrid name in the verbal imperative, making it untranslatable into most other languages. It was a large, perplexing structure with windows shaped like guitars or swollen, stunted crosses, or some biomorphic shape resembling the human head and neck; and it was the trophy, or vanity project, of a contemporary baron of the economy, a certain software giant named Paul G. Allen.[17]

It was also the place where my critical powers were suddenly daunted, as I tried to place it within the context of human life and community experience. Sophie and Peewee were stymied as well.

"It looks like it got hit by a giant eight-wheeler," Sophie joshed; and indeed, this twisted, bulbous carcass of steel—which

---

17. Our colorful and beloved multi-billionaire, film producer, philanthropist and co-founder of Microsoft, whose fun-loving nature led to the eventual ownership of both a football and basketball team and whose comments are continually amusing and inspiring us (e.g., "We've had some tough times, but we've hung in there."). Currently guiding some of the most innovative companies in the area, such as Vulcan Ventures, Inc., which "creates and advances a variety of world-class endeavors and high-impact initiatives that change and improve the way we live, learn, do business and experience the world."

I later learned had been crafted using a computer-generating technique also used to design Mirage fighter jets and pieced together out of 280 undulating ribs plastered with 21,000 irregularly shaped, riveted metal shingles, then painted in five colors, one of which was designated "Purple Haze"—did, irresistibly, bring to mind an accident.

"What an eyesore!" Sophie went on. "Here you have this beautiful Space Needle just a couple hundred feet away, and then you have this whatever it is!"

"It's Hendrix's guitar, smashed,"[18] suavely pontificated Peewee, which was what everybody said, since this museum was dedicated to the memory of the guitar-smashing acid-rock legend, who'd been a native of the city, a member of its miniscule African-American population.

I, however, knew better. I knew that this battered Moloch was actually a modern place of worship, a mangled Cathedral. That's why I wasn't the slightest bit surprised after entering its vaulted interior to find a great hall dubbed "The Sky Church" swooping to a height of 85 feet above our heads.[19] It commanded us into its sacred space and summoned us to tilt our heads back in awe and exaltation—at an Absence—a non-God.

It took me a while to realize that Sophie, Peewee and I were standing in one of the most brazen syntheses of the sacred and profane ever attempted: a museum of rock 'n' roll named and arched

18. Actually, Peewee's observation is approximately correct. From Clair Enlow, in *Architecture Week*: "The real inspiration for the project is a pile of trash gleaned from an electric guitar shop near [Gehry's] office in Santa Monica."

19. Cathedral, *Schmathedral*. It's just a reference to Jimi Hendrix's vision of a musical democracy, a "church" of the people. Chill out, Fortiphton.

like a church, built in honor of a dark-skinned, anarchist revolutionary, whose apocalyptic contempt for materialism and whose anti-nationalist beliefs, expressed publicly by the violent smashing of his own expensive guitar to the sound of ear-splitting music and a raucous, hallucinogenic parody of the national anthem, were now being rapturously exalted under the aegis of a high priest of venture capitalism—as a service to "community," and the captain of industry magnanimously commanded we worship.

Such a concept was, in all honestly, almost too much to take in. On the ceiling, like figures from the Sistine Chapel, swirled shifting images of American pop legends, an ever changing, ghostly procession, testament to the fact that a static pantheon of saints is no longer enough; one must have always new objects for one's adoration.

Through this chasm of exalted commerce regularly pierced the sleek monorail, like an arrow repeatedly penetrating the body of a crumpled Sebastian. But none of what I am saying conveys the yawning nihilism of the experience,[20] mixing exhibits applauding the architect's career with phosphorescent time capsules of musical accoutrements and a Jacob's Ladder of guitars stretching heavenward; and leaving us, poor Sophie, Pee-wee and myself, clutching my miserable bag of hair dye, like dazed flotsam on the perpetually swirling froth of culture, in this

---

20. Aren't the following—both from local writers I might add—clearer glimpses of the EMP: "Built in the midst of the Seattle Center, Experience Music Project looks like one of the crazy fun forest amusement park rides."—*Via: The AA Traveler's Companion*. "I learned Alanis Morissette's 'Thank U' on an electric piano whose lighted keys guided my noodling."—Kathryn Robinson, *Seattle Weekly*.

museum of natural history, temple of learning and ultimate abyss of the spiritual all in one—a cosmic marketing joke about a temple.

We walked with the feeling of having been diminished and silenced (an intended effect, I was sure), along a path littered with wet maple leaves toward the outmoded Space Needle, that World's Fair leftover, once the highest structure in town, the shape of which resembles a pagoda stretched out of proportion, with a vaguely rhomboid glass entrance hall at the foot, the irregular curves of the latter a sad attempt at emulating the mangled surface of the nearby Church of Rock 'n Roll. We passed glumly with a crowd of others into the Needle's elevator of burnished steel, in which we were fastidiously rearranged with an eye to greatest convenience upon exit by the loquacious operator, who had been highly trained as an information specialist and thereby combined blue and white collar in one downsized employee.

As we were swept smoothly upwards, we were informed in clear, ringing tones of several verities:

1) We were traveling at 10 miles per hour, 50% the speed of a "normal" elevator;

2) and being delivered to a restaurant precisely 500 feet above ground (if we possessed reservations);

3) and said restaurant, having been built in 1962, was therefore "the oldest revolving restaurant in the United States,"

4) where we would be subjected to exactly one complete revolution of the city every 7 minutes.

"What are we, supposed to be taking notes or something?" Peewee quipped defensively.

The revolving restaurant, dubbed Sky City, immediately produced a sensation of vertigo in him. However, since we had made reservations and shown up, they had our names and credit cards, and Sophie said it would be rude to ask for immediate exit from the revolutions without at least a snack; so we sat down and ordered (Sophie was excited about finding a dish that featured chanterelles and morels from the local forests); and then we ate wordlessly, still digesting the Cathedral of Musical Emptiness we had seen and experiencing our slow inching in a circular pattern.

Seattle looked still and molten from our perch by the window, the water of the bay and the sky above all one hardened color. "What a lovely battleship gray," I piped, unable to conceal my dark reveries. "That's what we have from now until April," instructed Sophie, flashing an abashed grin, but behind her head the sky suddenly betrayed tinges of purple of the shade found in the iridescences of a sharp blade. My eyes crept along the thin gray-blue line differentiating the Cascade Mountains from the horizon. "Peewee," I said, trying to sound jocular, "tell me about value, pleasure and danger in the Northwest."

"Keep your powder dry," he answered. "Invest in stocks."

The reference to "powder" provoked strange doubts in me about Peewee's macho image, but before I could pursue them, he was telling me that he and Sophie were making plans to leave the area, anyway. Despite the remoteness of their nest in Redmond, there was an element to fear here, which had crept in gradually over the years, virtually unnoticed by all save them. They had seen, apparently, some first cases of vandalism in a Starbucks parking lot not far along the highway from their home, and certain suspicious characters, with a look of miscegenation, had been filtering into the block.

"The neighborhood really isn't revitalized like they promised," offered Sophie, using that strangely effervescent term as a euphemism for "gentrified."

I knew for a fact that the population of the whole region was overwhelmingly white, because a certain Narcissa W. Applegate, a maven of one of the local historical societies and a sometime writer,[21] with whom I'd been corresponding by e-mail in my preliminary research, had sent me the statistics. Still, the dark shadow of race-mixing, dim as it was, seemed to have proved too much for my relatives, and specifically, Peewee, despite the fact that he hailed from Baltimore, and was not, in actuality, at all a Seattle type. Because scales of decadent cynicism had long ago encrusted my heart, I enjoyed seeing Peewee's blatant racism juxtaposed against the blank no-speak of the West, like a thundercloud on the steel-blue sheen of a Seattle sky.

"Yeah," he was elaborating, "a break-in just a mile away from us. And to think we came out West to get away from all that crap. I got a gun now, and I damn sure know how to use it. Not

---

21. A poor attempt at understatement at best. I'm the author of sixteen monographs on subjects of importance to this region that include texts on the first Spanish attempt to build a settlement at Nootka; the experiences of my great-great-aunt Narcissa Whitman, who was the first woman to cross the Oregon Trail; and conflicts between Methodists and Calapooia Indians in the education of children in 1839; not to mention pamphlets considering Canadian perspectives on the Pacific Northwest as actually being the Pacific Southwest, as well as the origin of the venereal diseases that decimated the Corps of Discovery under the aegis of Lewis and Clark.

for me, cause I can take care of myself, but if those scum was to try to hurt Sophie."

"Honey," cooed Sophie placatingly, with a glint of pride for her big strong hubby, "you know I can take care of myself. Why, it's almost exciting!" And Peewee fired a poisonous glance in her direction, as if to say, "slut."

Our conversation passed rather abruptly to tales of a millennium scan that Peewee's grandmother was about to undergo. This all-over body imaging, the blue-chip standard of magnetic resonance, could spy, Peewee rejoiced, into every millimeter of the human body. With this observation, his eyes flamed feverishly, in a way similar to those times he had discussed ferreting out the perpetrator in a case of criminal negligence. He seemed so caught up in the magic of this new invention that he barely heard my remark.

"Sounds like a millennium scam."

Sophie heard me and courageously tried to change the subject. Although she was aware of my interest in and occasional writings about underclass urban life, I think she was making a veiled reference to certain of my affairs that had scandalized the family when she chirped, "So, Uncle Reggie, you're with middle class people today. When do you see your underclass?"

"Oh, there's no hurry for that," I answered blandly. "I don't think they'll be leaving your city any time soon." This caused Peewee to dagger off another look—at me this time—as if to imply that I might be the one who'd taught the excitement-loving slut her nature.

That evening, the same young man from the publishing company who'd been my chauffeur from the airport came to take me to an opening at the contemporary art museum at the University of Washington.[22] He was with my "rival," his wife, a rather appealing, shy young lady whom I soon learned had a connection to the region's upper classes, and perhaps even hailed from one of their notable families; high-western, I'd call it, if pressed for a term.

Her slightly dazed eyes and nervous, giddy laugh, were propelled, I would later learn, by frequent indulgence in a particular herb; and at the gallery and other places we met, her state of consciousness completed the framework for a certain curiosity on my part, since it seemed to set her strangely aside—like a pop-out figure against a two-dimensional background—from the very carefully conscious members of the cultural bourgeoisie around us, all of whom seemed to possess the same special brand of alertness.

What this was is extremely difficult to put into words; but the group of people I was about to see at the gallery for which we were heading, and who would be dressed, almost down to the last, in natty, sober, designer, but often dowdy, black, projected neither the unbalanced distraction of the intellectual nor the bland, thoughtless conformism of typical middle class Americans. It wasn't just that bohemia was dead, as was the case all over the country, for something existed that belonged to this place alone.

As I searched for a word, all that came to mind was the insufficient adjective "careful," which didn't in the least do

---

22. The Henry Art Gallery at "U Dub," as we affectionately "dub" the University of Washington. Don't miss the campus if you're here in spring, when bulb flowers and azalea bushes provide a spectacular sight.

justice to the capable opaqueness within which each seemed enclosed and also wouldn't explain why it was so unsettling to me. "Guarded," perhaps, was an even less precise attempt, for at least on the surface, some were even garrulous, cordial.

Yet whatever it was, the smooth, laconic control projected from artists, amateurs of art and critics alike, which I assumed had replaced bohemian styles of the past, concealed something that was both an entitlement and a renunciation, some profitable form of compromise in some unspoken way that all understood. I watched my host's occasionally stuttering wife in her mildly hallucinogenic isolation, popping out from this background of well-oiled social behavior, and knew that her contrasting behavior held part of the key to my understanding of the place.

But I'm getting ahead of myself. In the car on the way to the gallery, I was, for a moment, uncharacteristically assertive, because I insisted that I must have a drink before I could walk into that museum. "I suffer," I explained, with a slight quaver in my voice, "from Stendahl Syndrome."[23] Understanding that the condition involved an overwhelming feeling of nausea and dizziness that occurs in museums and galleries as a result of an overload of culture, my young host quipped, "I'm sure they have a Stendahl Quarantine Station they can put you in at the gallery."

---

23. An apocryphal "medical" diagnosis, loosely adapted from Stendahl's description of seeing St. Croce, in Florence, in 1817, and experiencing palpitations of the heart in the face of such beauty. It's interesting to observe the author's notion of having brought up an original, fresh idea, when "Stendahl's Syndrome" has even lately become the title of a trashy thriller (1996) by Dario Argento, starring his daughter, Asia, and been experienced by Homer in a sequence of *The Simpsons*.

"What could it be?" piped up his wife, "An all-white tiled room with a hose?"

Half from a nervous need for chatter and half out of an intention to penetrate the psyche of this city, I asked the young couple to explain the enigma of Kurt Cobain to me. I knew it informed the minds of almost everyone of a certain age in this city, and Narcissa Whitman, my historical-society lady e-mail correspondent (whose communications sounded anything but youthful[24]), had even identified it as "a key to the youth culture of Seattle." I'd perused some video recordings of the rock star at the Museum of Film and Television before leaving the East and had been taken aback and unpleasantly mystified. I wanted my young hosts to deconstruct the nervous, dandyish personality I had seen projected in interviews, the many ringed fingers and the lisp that seemed to creep into the singer's voice as if it were intentional. "Was it anxiety?" I asked.

"Well, he thought of himself as bi," answered the wife.

His manner confused me, however, juxtaposed as it was with macho pogo-stick stage leaps and the gratuitous destruction of sound amps, which recalled fraternity misbehavior to me.

"You see, it was ironic," explained my male host. "He pre-broke all his amps and fit them together so they'd come apart easily. Then he'd put them back together later. They were too poor to replace them."

"But," I brooded politely, "all his personae seemed so artificial to me, whether it was punky rage or logger funk—do I have the terms right? It all had a peroxided, Hollywoodian feel."

---

24. No complexes and a healthy lifestyle make me more than happy to provide my age: forty-seven.

I thought I saw my hosts bristle a bit. "No," the husband recited, "he was a legitimately impoverished child of the Aberdeen depressed logging community."

"I'm not talking about roots, but his aesthetic," I insisted, perhaps a little too grumpily.

"It was all performance."

"But what in the world was his talent?"

"Provocateur, musician, talented antagonist," listed the husband emphatically as if to say, case closed.

I made a mental note to bring it up once more.

By the time we arrived at the gallery, I'd imbibed several doubtful cocktails at a bar that, strangely enough, doubled as a vegetarian restaurant. "Alcoholic vegetables," was the whimsical invention of my female companion by way of explanation. I hadn't enjoyed the experience a whit, because I'd been forced to retreat into the perpetual rain for every cigarette, in between which I chugged the drinks to keep up with my hosts, who always stayed inside.

The exhibit at the gallery, purported to have something to do with "fictive architecture," was astonishing in one respect only, for its seemingly meaningless images, and at first I struggled to think of the French science fiction film I'd once seen of which it reminded me.[25] Abandoned quite soon by my hosts, who seemed a little embarrassed to be caught in my presence, I strolled past some pink-and-salmon pastel squares of illuminated Lucite that looked more like interior decorating than sculpture to me and into a large, nearly empty room. The room was

---

25. Probably *Alphaville, une étrange aventure de Lemmy Caution*, dir. Jean-Luc Godard, 1965.

copiously illuminated, bringing to my mind thoughts of the clear light of reason, which, as I have explained, I have always associated with the Sun. But here there were only five black car tires, balanced on their edges, arranged equidistantly apart. The tires had been placed in an oblique relationship to the walls of the room, the way a good decorator might position a couch. Across the gleaming floor, which was of bleached wood that had been expensively tinted rose, marched groups of two or three visitors, who inevitably paused dutifully in front of the five parallel tires standing on edge and studied them carefully, their slightly compressed lips betraying almost no expression, except perhaps a touch of glumness.

The execution of this installation, I surmised, had merely entailed purchasing five new car tires and placing them on the floor at a pleasantly oblique angle, perhaps using glue or some other adhesive to keep them from rolling. The arrangement of the tires, combined with the periodic, serious and silent perusal of them—each instance of which seemed to be of identical duration (although that I may have imagined)—were the only thing going on in the large room.

Eventually the scene produced a stabbing pain in my chest and a simultaneous heaving of my alcohol-filled gullet. Fear regarding my lack of that critical faculty that would allow me, as well, to contemplate the tires for a specified serious duration and then move on forced me onto a desperate path of suppositions.

There was, of course, a geometric simplicity to the sight in front of me that recalled the classical and geometric proportions elucidated by the Ancients. But such a track of thought brought me no clue to the mystery of why a large room in a gallery had been given over to these five very common objects. All of it took the better part of an hour as I tried to analyze the ritual of gazed-upon tires by supposing that they were the result of the artist's subtle and considered meditation on the production of "commodifying signs." However, as I forced myself to keep staring at the tires and industriously considered this possibility, they continued to lack the visual seduction of anything one would normally associate with the distillation of commodifying signs, especially since artists of previous generations—from Duchamp with his urinal to Warhol with his soup cans—had already accomplished such a disjunctive vision in undeniably startling ways.

Beads of sweat appeared on my forehead as I struggled to decide whether the five tires were actually evocative of another kind of disjunction, perhaps relating to "appropriation"; that is to say, by removing the tires from their manufacturing plant, retail station or the floor of a Pep Boys garage and balancing them on end without connection to any other object, the artist had perhaps succeeded in some profound appropriation of them, thereby freeing them from their embedded context and ingeniously deleting the commodifying thrill that normally cast them in a hypnotic relationship to Spectacle—and thus revealing them as dead, meaningless objects that had deluded us. This would mean, however, that the series of black-clad onlookers who contemplated these five black tires for the specified period of absorption had formerly seen them only in their incarnation as thrilling objects for consumption; and now they were undergoing a revelation. For the first time, they were seeing these objects stripped of their illusory signifying power while I, less enlightened, stood on the sidelines in perplexity.

Yet this was difficult for me to believe, because on numerous occasions in my life I had easily been able to look at tires merely as dead objects drained of meaning, possibly because one often saw them in waste dumps or lying abandoned at the side of the road; and certainly it took only a small effort, if one felt compelled, to imagine these objects cleaner and standing on end in a row, in a gallery, for instance, without there being any need for some undeniably original artist to effect such an event. So I had to be wrong again.

Like a disabled individual deprived of an essential sense, I stood by the passing series of elect, voyeuristically envying the epiphanic transport I assumed was in their solemn stares, which pointed like sacred vectors in a religious painting at the hermetic revelation of the tires. I'd even gotten to a point of considering the possibility that the black-clad individuals were actually hired elements of the installation, paid to study it at intervals, and that I was the only one who hadn't been told about it.

Precisely at this point in my unpleasant meditation, a particular lone viewer, radiating a shocking vitality that could not have been the artificial charm of a paid actor, stopped before the arrangement of five at a moment when only the two of us shared this large room that had become the privileged space of the tires. Over his broad, square ivory forehead fell a lush shock of shiny sable hair, which he would blow away from his eyes with an occasional exhalation of his extended lower lip. Below that pouting lip jutted a classically proportioned jaw marred only by a deep, shadowy dimple, and all of it was balanced on a symmetrical, columnar neck that could easily have been mistaken for marble.

Despite the rainy, near freezing weather from which he must have just emerged, given the dampness of a loose tan tank top of rough raw silk that clung vaguely to the soft depression of a navel and two pert nipples, he wore only a pair of thin corduroy shorts that molded the swellings of two high buttocks; and as he raised an elongated arm of satin-encased muscle to push away the shock of hair because the exhalation had not fully succeeded, a gleaming cluster of armpit hair was revealed.

Upon seeing this conjunction of vitality with the stubbornly present, until then uninterpretable tires, a sudden, optimistic hope about finally understanding the installation overtook me; for he, too, was studying them with a curious respect, without having lost a smidgen of the hypnotic energy radiating from him. He was Mercury, arrived shining to bring me the message that would answer this riddle. His eyes locked with my questioning, pleading gaze, and I was struck with the certainty that, by some gift of providence, I was about to be initiated into the tire mystery.

"I've got six of those things sitting in my garage and I can just never throw them out," he pronounced. "Sure am glad somebody found something to do with 'em."

Sure am glad somebody found something to do with 'em! His interpretation produced a sudden, violent reaction, like a reel jerked into rewind, bringing in fast motion all the previous spectators backward into the room they'd left and making them part of the same revelation:

They were sure glad somebody found something to do with 'em!!!

Like a whirring mantra, the words impelled me in a run from the room, while images of the day spit through my brain like sparks from a Catherine wheel: the Void of Rock 'n Roll Emptiness; the Needle tortured higher like pulled taffy or carnival glass; the harsh congealed consommé of water, mountain and sky revealed by the windows of the revolving restaurant; and Five Black Tires All In A Row! Their inevitability was a carrousel that became a churning in my stomach; my steps sped even faster through the exit and into the rainy courtyard, where more clusters of the black clad stood in the naked light of a harsh spot; and there I vomited copiously in a corner, remembering the imaginary Stendahl Quarantine station, but thinking, no, I'm not overwhelmed by aesthetics, I'm over- or under-whelmed by the lack of them, and that's "Anti-Stendahl Syndrome!"

The place still held one more epiphany, however, and it came again in the form of the barely dressed young man with the unruly lock of hair, who, having probably strolled serenely out of the room of the Black Tires after my own rapid exit, was now standing with a group of friends in the courtyard as I lurked soiled in the shadows, wiping my mouth with the edge of a sleeve. In their thin black jackets they all seemed to be dressed too lightly for the chilly, damp weather; but he stood out among them, as much for the light color of his tank top as for his state of near undress, because his naked arms and smooth chest visible above the low scoop of his tank top glowed even more like marble in the harsh light.

He was talking blissfully, while others listened raptly, of his trip into the "wilderness," in which he had gone in quest of the perfect beach, camping on chilly shores where the temperature dropped to near freezing; walking barefoot on ice-cold, wet rocks. For this reason, he explained, he felt inured to the relatively higher temperature of the city, which was the reason for his fetchingly scant clothing on this chilly autumn night.

His blitzed-out monologue led me to think that the city, then, with its hills and bodies of water, was like a rollercoaster or funnel constantly expelling you toward Nature, urging some relationship to it even beyond your will.

Already having seen the small park with its funereal billboards about the defeat of nature by industry and commerce, I knew that urban life tolled the death knell for the vision of nature toward which the city spilled; but the youthful inhabitants of this city seemed caught in a perpetual conflict between urban life and some Wordsworthian delight of the countryside. Which must have been why the young man seemed to be in an altered state. The bliss of nature for these inhabitants was a kind of drug abuse, which they were compelled to repeat over and over again, returning from it in their altered state that left them impervious to temperature. And I began to wonder how many addicts this had claimed among the local young.

III

An Entitlement and a Renunciation

"All that comes to mind is the insufficient adjective 'careful,' which doesn't explain why it's so unsettling to me," I said to my young chauffeur, albeit a bit too stiffly and too academically for my usual pose.

In another excess of generous hosting, my Alpine-blond host, the one who'd picked me up at the airport and taken me to the gallery, was now speeding me all the way south to Portland. There I'd meet the editorial head of these operations, the publishing company's creative flame and a figure of some renown on the local literary scene, Machu Stapler. "Machu," my young host obligingly explained, not due to any exotic ethnicity, but because his parents had been close friends with America's first ecologist and author of *Silent Spring*, Rachel Carson, and wanted their son to embody the spirit of that paradisiacal Incan setting. Machu Picchu, the discovery of which led to slaughter and to the current deplorable anti-ecological state of things.

I knew I was supposed to be observing the terrain as we headed out of the city, but after a short time, my eyes felt glazed by the bland sight of just another superhighway, so out of sync with the thought of that mountain jungle high above the cloud forest evoked by my editor's name. We could have been practically anywhere in America.

More on my mind was the formal, detached tone my speech had suddenly adopted. It may seem strange that the rhetoric of the notes I'd been scribbling had leaked into my social discourse; but truth is, the shock of the gallery experience had jolted me into a kind of masochistic submission. I felt partially cowed, although I suspected I'd rally again in my cynicism. In the meantime, however, and in a desperate attempt, I suppose, to fade into the social fabric of the place, I was hoping to ape the mysterious politeness of the natives. Being, as usual, totally inept on the level of ordinary intercourse, I found my speech mutating instead into a kind of literary impersonality. It was the closest I could come to the detached mode of conversation I thought I was supposed to have here; which was itself, as a matter of fact, the subject of our current conversation.

"Why are people in Seattle so guarded?" my companion lamented rather theatrically, in another obvious attempt at bonding, raising a hand from the wheel to stroke a smooth jaw that held just a few hairs. "Never wanting to seem rude and never committing."

By some occult reflection, he was, for me, also reproducing the very phenomenon we were discussing. I'd been puzzled, even abashed, by the strange feeling of vacancy around the gestures of the gallery people, who, even when garrulous, seemed to be following some formula of crafty etiquette, but I was just as stymied by the current phenomenon of the two of us in the car; because in contrast to my evasively literary manner of expression, I was drooling quite blatantly through hooded eyes at his nonchalantly parted thighs, feeling even more unbridled now that my rival, his wife, wasn't there.

Earlier, as we'd studied a map together in the front seat, its pages spread across both our laps, I'd even given in to the impulse of letting the back of a concealed hand stray against one of those fairly youthful thighs (I'd already paid the price for other thighs of a much, much more youthful nature, and I could still sense the irritation caused by that ankle guard). My gesture hadn't in the least interrupted the flow of his speech, unless it was the cause of a sudden, slight twitch. And now, rapacious as the expression pasted on my face indubitably was, it continued to produce no effect upon him.

It occurred to me for a moment that his apparent lack of discomfort, his non-acknowledgment of the moves I was so obviously making, could have been a foolproof regional technique used to repulse unwelcome advances; but this didn't explain where those who practiced this technique got the extraordinary sangfroid needed to maintain it. So I chalked it up to one more example of that bland impenetrability that characterized the behavior of the people, and I hovered on the edge of an actual pounce.

"People smile," my host was musing, "but there's no depth or warmth." The back of my hand was actually touching his thigh by now, the knuckles drumming softly against it, but he heeded it not at all. "They aren't invited over to their friends' homes very often," he went on obliviously. "Everybody feels like they're being kept out of some level of activity. And there you have it."[26]

---

26. Either this conversation has been completely fabricated or the speaker leads a shadow life in Seattle. I myself was a recent witness to the ebullience and outgoing nature of many Seattlers when the Columbia Historical Legion and the Daughters of the Oregon Trail Historical Committee came together in Redmond for a joint fund-raiser. Hilarious one-legged races, playful parodies of some of our local officials, not to mention a highly effective monologue by a young actress playing the part of Narcissa Whitman undergoing the most arduous moments of the Oregon trail, created a personal, candid atmosphere at which every single person had fun. No one's being kept out.

For a moment it occurred to me that my host might merely be expounding upon a kind of behavior typical of white bourgeois Anglo-Saxon sensibility,[27] and that his seeming inability to label it as such was due to the fact that he was a member of that ethnicity and didn't have the distance to identify it. This didn't, however, explain the cryptic tone of the behavior we were trying to analyze, its seeming lack of response to certain stimuli—all of it as mysterious as his refusal to acknowledge my hand on his thigh—a parallel suggesting that each and every practitioner of this behavior belonged to a society of secret signals and signs of an archaic Masonic flavor.

"The way these people behave," I offered, once again astonished by the professorial tone of my own voice, "does perplex me. Perhaps it's a sense of entitlement. Yet there's a form of 'renunciation' that occurs at the same time." It was as if each of the bearers of this secret code had agreed not to step on another's toes nor claim too much—in order to be granted some unholy power or mastery, which brought with it spoils of every sort. What I couldn't yet understand was whether the practitioners felt satisfied or stifled by their sacrifice.

"Seattle thinks of itself," answered my young host, who seemed to reduce the angle of his parted thighs almost imperceptibly, causing my hand to drop onto the seat with a light thump, "as the commercial capital of this region. Since the people who flock to it are hoping for upward mobility, they tend to be a little guarded."

"But people come to brash, aggressive, over-expressive New York for the same reason," I wheedled.

---

27. Another example of the author's reverse racism—a virtual obsession for him.

"More people," was all he mumbled, and I instinctively knew he meant that this city wasn't chaotic enough to allow the social risk-taking of a New York. Perhaps here it was the proverbial one-bad-move-and-you're-out. On the other hand, there didn't even seem to be any chance for the right or wrong "move." There was a kind of social isolation.

My host had moved back to a more rewarding train of tutorial thought: Nirvana. Obviously, my terse remarks of the previous night had stuck a bit in his craw and he needed to settle the score. "What you don't understand," he said, about to use a weighty metaphor for something that seemed little more than a passing trend, "is that a lot of the people who won the *grunge mantle*[28] were upper middle class suburbanites who could penetrate the city's guarded nature and had enough security to construct irony." The word *irony*[29] set off a bell in my head, like the word

28. "Grunge," indeed. Hired to write a useful guide to our region, the author keeps swerving off into subcultures whose importance to our community is minor. Rough guides into the underbelly of a place have their value, but not when presented under the false pretense of an in-depth study. Don't expect any investigation of Seattle's innovative digital industries nor even any information about its vital institutions of higher learning and art; just furtive, demoralized accounts of its cultural hangers-on and other insignificant marginals.

29. There are a surfeit of books and articles claiming to skewer this region for supposed humorlessness or lack of irony, the majority of them written, of course, by east-coasters. Don't believe the hype. A casual sampling of Seattle's nightlife, for example, will reward you with high-quality comedy clubs and two nationally acclaimed theater companies that specialize in political satire. Co-existent with these supercilious appraisals from know-it-all critics are a breed of new films and books exploiting Seattle's very contemporary comic sensibility, such as the superb *Sleepless in Seattle*.

water occurring to Dorothy in the Wizard of Oz. I made a mental note to make use of it in case of emergency.

"Speaking of irony," I said in my first reconnaissance into this new territory, "is there any?"

He didn't answer, for we were already pulling up to Machu Stapler's Victorian house. The plan was for me to pick up the car he was offering and get my itinerary, which, strangely enough, had been kept secret from me.

Perhaps it was the lurid gold of the maple leaves in fall on this surprisingly sleepy street that gave it a Hansel-and-Gretel feeling, or was it the house, with its child-friendly yet aggressive colors of designer granny-apple green, chalky wisteria and hot plum, its multicolored house number made from wire bent to resemble a child's scrawl; or perhaps still it was the smile of welcome on Machu Stapler's face, which could have been mistaken for a leer.

The mouth was moving, as well—I soon realized, as I fought for perception through my squeamish daze—and making an ambiguous pleasantry about not letting me into his house while I was smoking, wondering jocularly how that habit had even allowed me entrance to the state of Oregon. I had just enough time to offer a clammy handshake, and Stapler shut the door again, while I stayed outside in the drizzle to finish my beloved Nat Sherman, blinking in the Halloween glare of the yellow maple leaves and taking deep, smarting inhalations of smoke into my lungs.

Through the window, confusedly overlaid by the garish mosaic outside, two unblinking blue eyes were staring. At first, I couldn't identify their species; then slowly, through the double exposure of the bright outside and dark interior, the outlines of a pink, childish face took form. Stapler's three-year-old son, no doubt. They were the first eyes of the trip to rest upon me with such candid curiosity, and I stared back at them dumbfounded and apprehensive, like an animal in a cage. He was watching in total absorption the movement of my hand each time it brought the cigarette to my mouth and each time a stream of smoke resulted from the gesture. Surrounded by careful, health-conscious protectors, in a region where it is against the law to bring your child with you to a bar and where smoking is forbidden in almost every other public place, never before perhaps had he seen this practice, outside of television. The thought of this possibility suddenly consumed me with resentment, which must have been the reason why, after my next inhale, I aimed an enormous cloud of smoke directly at the window.[30] When it cleared, those penetrating oglers, the eyes, were happily gone, and this filled me with an uncanny faith in the ability of my portable smokescreen to distill all adversaries. But I still had to face the editor. Stubbing out my butt inside the Halloween pumpkin on the porch railing, I timidly knocked.

---

30. Maybe these repeated bizarre and silly gestures of aggression against children aren't so surprising. I've been reluctant to bring this information into the text. Although I tried to think of it as irrelevant, the seeds of infraction seem to be present already in this seemingly innocuous anecdote. It is time, I feel, to point out a prior conviction that I researched after having my suspicions raised. Especially since the author is out of state, away from the local registry that would label him as such. On March 4, 2000, Fortiphton was, I regret to report, charged with four counts of criminal behavior—and one of them for administering an intoxicating agent to a minor. Am I being overly vigilant? One can't be too careful.

Certainly the door was swung open rather enthusiastically by Stapler. His clothing was nondescript: a shapeless sweatshirt over a half-tucked-in flannel shirt, worn jeans; but one's eyes were quickly drawn away from the body, as if it were saying, you'll be bored here, and summoned rather imperiously toward two of the most quizzical eyebrows I'd ever seen. Beneath them was a vital, piercing gaze, as impersonal as a laser, and lower down was that ambiguous smile I'd noticed first off, formed by attractive, curvaceous lips, that suggested, I surmised, though perhaps incorrectly, playful cruelty.

Why, I wondered, did I suddenly feel as if I were standing at the entrance to something cavernous and unknown, about to hear an elegy to "children of the night"? I nervously tried to peek around the mass of his body to spot the child, but he was nowhere in sight. Then I was drawn again to that glazed glance, a gaze that seemed to take everything about me in at once, with a placid reptilian registry. But there was something else about it as well, and it was—a gaze of entitlement and renunciation.[31]

Again I was seized by the feeling that there had suddenly been a tightening of that transparent membrane that shrouds

31. Fortunately for readers, I'm quite familiar with the editor sullenly described in this sequence. I can assure you that Machu Stapler is a pillar of this community who was instrumental, among other things, in the construction of the sorely needed new Seattle library, designed by the renowned architect, Rem Koolhaas. He has also reinvigorated the literary scene of our region with numerous selfless contributions to readings, fledgling magazines and book discussion groups about the work of young writers. Why has he taken on such a grim, imperative and shadowy persona in these pages? Maybe it's merely a sign of the first stages of this author's mental confusion.

everything, giving some slack at every gesture only to snap back resiliently to its original wall-like state. Like a small child (and indeed, the other was there, sitting on the floor, surrounded by plastic toys in primary colors, ignoring me), I battered against it, letting out quips and cynicisms that would have offended any other human. Compulsively I satirized the previous evening at the gallery, belittled the grim drive from Seattle to Portland, re-dubbed the lodgings that had been found for me "Hotel Hiroshima." But to no avail, for none of it had any effect upon the impenetrable cheerfulness of Stapler, whose clear, unflinching eyes never lost their bright, impervious surveillance, boring into me, showing no annoyance but offering a total lack of compassion when I said, "My feet are so cold." And this was the moment when the child, who'd given an impression of being totally absorbed in his plastic toys on the floor, suddenly revealed that he'd been listening to the entire conversation and stared at my frigid feet with a gloating air. He rose, floated over to the thermostat, which was set for 62, and moved it down to 60.

Machu Stapler was holding a sealed envelope. "Here's your itinerary."

"Don't you want to discuss some of the places, tell me what you're looking for? I need an angle. And what about directions?"

From the clutter of plastic milk cups, discarded toys and cereal bowls on the kitchen table, my editor pinched the corner of a roadmap between thumb and forefinger and gingerly held it forth. "It's all here."

"OK! But what about point of view?!"

"Yours will be enough."

I was breaking down. "Um… you know, perhaps I haven't been that honest with you."

"Sounds delightful." The constant smile had now truly become a leer. I heard the rumble of my bags being moved from the car outside by the Alpine blond.

"The weather has me terribly congested. And headachy. You wouldn't happen to have something strong, some codeine, would you?"

The child gazed unabashed at me, with wide curious eyes, as if I were an after-school special.

"You don't have any codeine and hypodermic syringes for our guest, do you Noah?" Stapler said playfully to the child. Then he flashed me a cutting grin to signal that he was indulging in fatherly banter. "Our friend gave Noah a play doctor's kit for his third birthday. There are plenty of plastic hypodermics scattered all over the house. But what about you, do you?"

"Do I what?"

"Have any opiatcs. I simply adore them. I love the feeling of, say, hydrocodone. I can read for hours on it."

"Read?"

He nodded—should I say the word?—ironically. "And I'd heard you were an admirer of the substance."

My heart sank to my knees. How much did he know? Maybe I'd underestimated their research skills. They'd looked into me, and probably the most bloodthirsty had been that consultant they'd sicked on me, that Heatherette Applegate-Whitman dame.[32] Mad as it was, my thoughts cartwheeled through the incidents of the last two days, reinterpreting everything as part of a big conspiracy. Perhaps that was it: the noncommittal glances, the mysterious reticence. They knew about me. They were all acting.

---

32. Correction: Narcissa Whitman Applegate. No hyphen.

"Opiates? Everything I have is by prescription," I said with a prudish clearing of the throat. "Maybe you should ask your doctor?"

Stapler's face screwed up into a supercilious mask that was purely satirical. "My *doctor*." The child let out a single peal of laughter that sounded like a shriek.

My editor led me to a battered Chevy. "Places to stay have been arranged for you all along the way," he cooed, as if facetiously comforting a hysterical child. "Just call if you need to push ahead any dates."

Suddenly he had the air of a grave guru as he opened the car door for me and the Alpine blond, who'd collected my bags from the other car, loaded them into the trunk.

At the sight of the interior, I gasped. The inside was sordid beyond imagining, the floor littered with squashed fast-food Styrofoam containers, balled tissues, straws still stuck into soft-drink-cup lids, a couple of smashed dolls' heads, an empty oilcan and a dirty bottle of antifreeze. The refuse crept up from the floor to cover the passenger seat next to me. Gasping at the stifling combination of odors, I stuck my head out the window on the driver's side. "What if it breaks down?"

Like Glenda the Good Witch and her sequin-shedding wand, Stapler magically produced a card from the shirt pocket under his sweatshirt. "Voila!" It bore the Automobile Club insignia and had their number.

IV

The Road to Croatan

Have I mentioned how much I detest cars? They're partly responsible for the depressing social disconnection in which we're all involved but that only I seem to admit. Cars are encapsulated, moving prisons. They became indispensable, of course, after World War II, with the growth of suburban life, as families fled the chaotic interactions imposed by the city. Little did they realize that cars were transporting them to "camps," secure enclosures that would implant them within a single tyranny bound by blood. Now cars exist only to prolong the cohesion of that nuclear unit, that perverse receptacle of Freudian family romance that has come to dominate every aspect of our culture, political life and geography. They transport mom, dad and kids from one regimented atmosphere to another, isolating them from chance encounters, prolonging and maintaining the enclosed microcosm of their resentful existence, offering only the possibility of a fatal accident as a way out of the script.

Like a phlegm-speckled throat, the engine that had been assigned me wheezed south into yet another one of those mad networks of vectors of force, which pits citizen against citizen and is known as a highway. Was this, I speculated, the wonderland of new culture that Stapler thought I could portray? Or did he think of this drive as a meaningless interlude, an unconscious state between two poles of signification, two kingdoms of Oz, punctuated as it was with bad local radio broadcasts, unhealthy fast food chains and road rage?

As I've already indicated, automobiles leave from nowhere and take you nowhere. They're metal capsules moving prisoners from the living room to the shopping mall, isolating them from any unpredictable social encounter save a road accident. They are the supply vehicles for sites sealed against variety and adventure.

Such were the thoughts that kept repeating themselves as I perched on the spring-broken seat of my own shoddy "cell," squinting through the interminable drizzle that veiled the Sun of reason, wondering about this raging alienation that had mushroomed inside me into an uncontrolled paranoia. Those jokes about the drugs. They had to know!

Defiantly, but with great anxiety, I used one hand to pop open the plastic pill case hiding in my pocket, raised two morphine pills to my lips, and swallowed them, without water. They stuck for one terrifying moment against the back of my throat, but with an exaggerated swallow I was able to force them down. I felt them hanging on a tonsil before they slid away, safe on their journey through my esophagus.

I heaved a sigh of anticipated relief and tipped a cigarette from the pack of Nat Shermans on the seat next to me. By my fifth smoke, the pills would be taking effect. Soon waves of numbed exhilaration would spread through my body, carrying away with them nagging worries. And after all, the little joke about opiates must have been pure coincidence; no one knew about the Mexican pharmacy from which I got monthly supplies of morphine through the Internet, least of all these new employers. They couldn't.

The waves came as predicted as I crushed out the fifth cigarette in the ashtray, the only space in the car that wasn't yet brimming with refuse. I fell into automatic pilot and imagined who the majority of others on this regimented force field were likely to be. Their minds must have been empty of everything, I surmised, except the programmed goals they'd inherited almost as surely as their genes. They were rushing past me with no real reason for speed, gaining a minute of extra time only to lose it again, accomplishing nothing but a dangerous state of competitive chaos that might transform this geometric system into something mangled and bloody: blank-faced housewives headed back from Home Depot with shrewd, determined eyes, their back seat loaded with fitted storage bins; spreading businessmen with pursed mouths, grimly expecting a predictable evening at home; pasty teenage boys in a desperate bid for an autonomous experience, hoping that their fake i.d. would get them into a porn shop on the strip mall; electricians and other small contractors in vans, enveloped in the gloom of unpaid bills and too many children.

I'd become a pawn, it occurred to me, in *their* plan, for it was powerful enough to engulf anyone found in its geographic pale. I must head in the direction of their lanes with my seatbelt buckled against a hefty fine, refresh myself with their roadside cuisine, inhale their pollution into my lungs. And for what? Merely to preserve this system of individual units composed of atoms of the nuclear family, joined together into the monotonous anatomy of this society.

Not one of these fools, it seemed, could sense the unhealthy, hothouse atmosphere of the contemporary suburban model. Mom, dad and siblings shut up in one Ethan Allen space that extended its bathetic isolation to a rectangular, manically attended lawn or an encapsulated steel unit known as a car. The acting out of phony pastoral dramas of security and decency, originally drawn from liberal conversations about child-raising in Victorian drawing rooms. Wasn't anyone aware that the incestuous urges, Oedipal hostility and sepulchral disciplines of family life could only implode if they were kept in such an isolated state? Didn't anyone but me miss the glory days of public transportation and public space when the city was indeed a spectacle to walk through and provided the *flâneur* his wonderfully tainted bath?

It was strange, but the old days of less mobility, when families, including grandparents, aunts, cousins and uncles, all lived for generations in the same town, had offered many unofficial opportunities for variety and experimentation that were now gone. The extended family had soothed and defused the Oedipal drama, often offering an alternative in the form of of an artistic spinster aunt or ribald uncle to those oppressed by small-minded parents. And as I've already explained, each member of the household, whether he or she could drive a car or not, from an activity as minor as buying a hat, was subjected to the colorful terrain of "downtown," that descendant of the Roman Forum.

Nowadays, the term "increased mobility" had become a ruse. It was about the movement of the next generation from one curtailed space into another, eating at a Denny's or mammalian Hooters that is exactly the same but in another location, producing a new family unit in another town bound by the same suspicion, resentment and fear.

Nevertheless, this imperfect molecule—the nuclear family—

was still being touted as the building block of our society, by the Right and Left alike; and because it's atoms are so secretly volatile and the space in which they circulate so curtailed and uniform, we were moving through life like a blindfolded person balancing a grenade, wrapping our claustrophobia and anxiety in the cotton batting of wholesomeness and civic concern, sublimating them into petty worries involving helmets for tricycle riders, low-fat menus and no smoking signs (as our SUV's belched smog into each other's lungs), until they would explode in large scale in the context of international conflict. Only then did our rage burst fully forth, played out with provincial contempt for other civilizations in scenarios of war and torture, until the infantilism of our position was revealed to all nations.

I'd been promised, however, an alternative to this oppressive monotony, a true and uncompromising opposition to it, in, of all places, the town for which I headed: Eugene, Oregon, a minor city of little more than 126,000, nestled in the hills at the southern end of the Willamette Valley at the place where two major tributaries join the Willamette River. In this apparently placid town, just east of the blue-collar suburb of Springfield in which many residents still work for a dying timber industry, and surrounded by hay farmers in the southern Willamette Valley, secret networks of subversive ecological activists were supposedly swarming. What was interesting was how clues to this disruptive presence had been imparted to me. Stapler had remained true to that stunning, almost contemptuous neutrality I'd just witnessed in the flesh by offering only a few offhand comments about the radical culture of

Eugene.[33] Whether this laconic approach to information stemmed from a wish to leave me at liberty to form my own impressions, or from a strange prudishness on his part or, perhaps, simply from chronic sloth when it came to performing his duties, I couldn't tell. I'd received only two emails from him on the subject, with website addresses pasted in, all of which pointed to essays by a certain primitivist-nihilist-Edenist-Luddite named John Zerzan. But I had no clue as to whether these expressed the political views of my editor; and furthermore, when I'd written that Applegate frump[34] about Eugene, querying her about Zerzan,

33. Again and again the author neglects real culture in favor of his fetishistic preoccupations. Enough already! I owe it to the reader to offer a more balanced introduction to this lovely and cultural city, which also happens to be the setting for the University of Oregon, the state's most important center of learning and largest campus. It's true that the city has a reputation for leftist politics, drug culture, etc., but such people represent a mere fragment of this optimistic burg, which had already become a railway hub and trading center by the latter half of the nineteenth century. Parks, galleries, flower gardens and museums abound; restaurants offer sophisticated cuisine in beautiful surroundings, and several coffee houses delight with their informal musical programs. Yes, a few radicals have entrenched themselves here since the 1960s, but the majority of these have mellowed and are now the owners of health-food stores, bookstores and other businesses of advantage to the community. So, please, I beg of you, don't let the author's sordid focus keep you from visiting one of the most delightful little cities in the Pacific Northwest.

34. Quite a presumption, since he's never met me. In compliance with the truth, which is of importance to anyone researching a travel document, I feel I must provide the information that I'm captain of the Willamette Women's Volleyball league, well within my weight range for my height, and though sporty, can generally be seen in slacks and tops from the Ralph Lauren or Liz Claiborne line.

she'd avoided the subject awkwardly, supplying instead bland copy that could have come from any two-bit tourist board.[35]

Consequently, I'd done my own legwork, discovering that Zerzan's thinking had influenced the Unabomber's manifesto,[36] but that it went beyond any rejection of industrialization or technology. No, Zerzan was such an ultra-primitivist that he thought he was leading an attack on symbolic thought, number and time themselves. His critique of civilization went all the way back to the moment when hunters and gatherers, whom he thought were in spontaneous ecstatic bonding with nature and the moment, turned to farming, thereby developing the eventual need for number, language and other aspects of symbolic representation. From there the movement toward social control, emotional repression and hierarchical structures was inevitable, according to him. Zerzan saw our hunting-and-gathering past as a lost but not unrecoverable Eden, and actually believed we could regress to a state when, in his own words, "reified time, language… number, and art had no place, despite an intelligence fully capable of them."[37]

---

35. If *Covered Wagon Women: Diaries and Letters from the Western Trails, 1852; Historical Atlas of the Pacific Northwest: Maps of Exploration and Discovery; A Window on Whaling in British Columbia;* and *"Some Seed Fell on Good Ground": The Life of Edwin V. O'Hara* sound like "bland copy" from a "two-bit tourist board," then I'll eat my Puget Sound oysters.

36. Unabomber's (Ted Kaczynski) *Industrial Society and Its Consequences* was allegedly influenced by the writings of John Zerzan. I recommend neither that text nor any of Zerzan's, most of which are absurd "back-to-nature" tracts, propped up by allusions to the work of various postmodern thinkers.

37. This and subsequent quotations of Zerzan's words are from "Future Primitive," by John Zerzan.

He went so far as to deplore every aspect of contemporary culture, tracing it back to cultivation and mastery of the land; and he felt that control of nature had led to the enslavement of others, not to mention alienation, ennui and pollution. From the very beginning of this process of the curtailment of liberty, language had "acted as an 'inhibiting agent." In other words, civilization had a stranglehold on life, damming off the flood of images and sensations that were characteristic of pre-modern consciousness. When communion with nature was prevented, "overlordship" and the taming of nature resulted. Thus, in Zerzan's eyes, a loss of every kind of human freedom went hand in hand with the development of symbolic thought. And astonishingly, he felt that language was no necessity for thought, but only a perverse turn of the cognitive process. He dispensed with it by saying that "because we actually think in language; there is no conclusive evidence that we must do so."

Even ritual, which most of us associate with early cultures, took on sinister implications in Zerzan's thinking: "The start of an appreciation of domestication, or taming of nature, is seen in a cultural ordering of the wild, through ritual. Evidently, the female as a cultural category, viz. seen as wild or dangerous, dates from this period." Art was also one of his bugaboos. He maintained that it had arisen almost directly from ritual, alienating us further from true, immediate contact with natural processes. As a futurist, Zerzan envisioned a world in which language, counting, art and all other forms of symbolic representation would no longer be necessary. Life would be spontaneous, nature would become an immediate reality and source of sustenance and shelter; human gatherings would arise spontaneously and festively, doing away with planned architecture or organized cities.

He was calling for nothing less than a return to the earth, which would eventually entail the abandonment of cities and all consolidations of power. He believed that historical time itself was the imposition of symbolic thought upon the ecstatically eternal moment, bringing with it sameness, repetition and convention. Thus, our notion of time would be abolished, too. And he saw all of it happening rather swiftly, without ever mentioning the word "revolution," although he didn't disdain the destruction of private property as a means to an end. The perpetrators of the new "un-order" would be certain youthful marginals, some of whom were probably in contact with him.

The cranky extremity of his theories and rejection of contemporary life amused me, and I tried to imagine him in a self-constructed hut, stubbornly upholding a subsistence lifestyle. In fact, I was fascinated by the thought of how he managed to reconcile his daily activities with his ideals. Obviously, he still used language and was engaged in quite a high level of symbolic thought. But did he get his food by gathering nuts in the forest? Did he write on a computer or scratch his thoughts into stone? Did he have a car? Did he buy clothes? In short, was he existing as nearly as possible to the manner of those first members of the English colony at Roanoke, who disappeared without a trace to live with a local Indian tribe and left only the inscription "gone to Croatan"?

Several attempts to contact Zerzan had proved fruitless; yet if truth be told, it was the periphery of youthful adherents to his ideas who interested me more than him. Many of these very young[38]

---

38. Bingo! Fortiphton reveals the real motives for his interest in Zerzan here. It's quite obvious, isn't it, given his record as an offender?

self-styled anarchists, whom Zerzan saw as a ray of hope for a future free of symbolic thought and social alienation, were rumored to be living in and around the city of Eugene. In fact, one of them, Jeffrey Luers, had made national news by setting fire to numerous Suburban and Tahoe SUV's at the car dealership Romania Chevrolet in Eugene, in June 2000, in order to bring attention to the global warming caused by these gas guzzlers. He'd received a 22-year prison sentence as a result. Many reviled people like Luers, but some were reminded of the Wobblies, West coast activists who rode the rails in the early 1900s in an attempt to unionize loggers.

The opiates prolonged their soothing embrace, entwining my body with filigrees of caressing warmth, blurring my resentment and transforming it into imperturbable harmony with the movement of the car. Maybe I was in that state that Zerzan described when he talked about the absence of number and time, supplanted by a deliciously trembling present, when the veil of symbolic thought (which I myself had already described as a gelatinous, imprisoning social membrane between myself and the warmth of the sun) was rent. I saw the anarchist boys[39] with their scraggly hair and generous doe-eyes, and began to wonder about Zerzan's sex life, for in none of his writings could I find

---

39. Categorically absurd, devious and delusional! Fortiphton's wishful thinking associates anarchism with males only. He should be informed that right here at the University of Oregon itself, as recently as 2001, Audrey Vanderford, a female instructor, offered a course entitled *Anarchafeminism*, an in-depth commentary on revolution, power, violence, sexuality and autonomy from a female, feminist point of view.

any reference to sexuality.[40] Was it, as well, a kind of symbolic expression that would be shorn of meaning and exist only for the purpose of procreation? Such were the questions I yearned to ask the young anarchists. I'd hypnotize them with my expressions of trust and patient smiles, maybe spend the night with them in some encampment or commune. But where would I find them?

Some, I knew, were still supposed to be perched in trees, outside Eugene in nearby Fall Creek, having their food lifted to them by pulley systems that brought their excrements back down. They endured inclement weather and the threats of rangers, police and tear gas for the purpose of calling attention to the destruction of old-growth forests and the dangers of clear-cutting. In Fall Creek, the controversy revolved around old-growth trees in a portion of the forest known as the Clark timber sale, which had totaled 94 acres in 1991. Conservationist activists, who claimed the cutting of the trees—some as old as 500 years—would further destroy the habitat of the endangered spotted owl, had tried to block the sale. Loggers, some of whom wore tee-shirts jocularly calling for the frying of the owl, vehemently disagreed. So the activists began hunting out the location of tiny mammals known as red voles, who live in the canopies of the trees, feasting on fir needles. Because they're a primary delicacy for the dwindling species of the spotted owls, they, too, are protected by a rare-species law. By the time the activists had staked out most of the red voles in the area and marked official buffers of safety around them (marking them, as well, of course, for slaughter by the spotted owl), the Clark timber sale had been reduced to a mere 29 acres. Meanwhile, the tree-sitters continued

40. As I have warned…

their stand-out, hoping that the now greatly reduced timber sale would discourage the lumber companies.

A lot of these eco-anarchists were involved in the newsletter *Green Anarchy*, which seemed to be edited primarily by Zerzan and had featured an essay by the Unabomber. Still others were supposedly camping out near the Willamette River, touting their homelessness as a symbol of their refusal to enrich the real estate monopoly.

Like a predator enlivened by the abject aggression of oppressed creatures, I made these boys come alive in my mind, their gangling adolescent limbs, their ratty sweatshirts that lifted to expose lean vegetarian bellies as they climbed from their sleeping bags, their melon-like buttocks that protruded like those of a monkey as they scrambled up trees. Now wouldn't they make a nice reference point for my research?[41]

First, however, I decided to follow my niece Sophie's counsel and give myself a more youthful look with the Winsome Wheat hair coloring she'd pressured me into buying. But even before that, I just had to see downtown Eugene. I wondered how many of the old nineteenth-century buildings from its years as a trading center were still standing. Certainly an authentic, old western city was a perfect inspiration for these young activists I'd been reading about, given that they were so nostalgic for a time of pre-globalization.

The morphine sent its swirling vapor through my brain cells, revealing at the center of its spinning cone an idyllic urban vision: those old downtown streets, candy stores and luncheonettes and

---

41. Need I say more?

a department store that bore the name of one of the old families of the city; and through the streets walked young, committed revolutionaries, in tune with the rhythms of the city, full of libido and energy and compassion for the city's oppressed minorities. I was coming off the freeway ramp to the East 6th Avenue exit of Eugene, but instead of heading for the motel further west on that street, I made a u-turn and drove east on 6th Avenue toward the downtown area.[42]

There was no there there.[43] "Downtown" seemed to be a vast gentrification project, its surviving landmark building occupied by an upstairs gym with windows overlooking the street. There were no pedestrians and just a few sluggish cars cruising by on the periphery.

I parked my car and wobbled out, a rush of opiates swirling through me. The center of downtown itself, that hallowed space that once teemed with representatives from every class and ethnicity, had been replaced by a large, sterile mall, and with a sinking heart, I strolled through it. As is almost always the case with these structures, the ceiling of every shop was exactly the same height, the windows and frontages devised according to a numbingly simple equation, and the majority of stores no more connected to the production of the region than they were any-where else in this country, although some were disguised to look like they were. On 5th Street, Eugene's "Market," once an old mill, was now merely another boutique mall, featuring the

---

42. He's driving the wrong way on a one-way street! Sixth Avenue in Eugene runs one-way only, in a westerly direction. Obviously, he's intoxicated!

43. Gertrude Stein's comment, upon revisiting her hometown of Oakland, CA, after years of expatriation in Europe.

"Heritage Nike Store"; and the closest old hotel standing was in exile at the edge of the downtown area.

I later learned from the only people on the street, a small, sullen knot of suburban punks crouching on the sidewalk in front of a closed convenience store to roll a couple of joints, that most of Eugene's old downtown had been torn down in the 1960s and replaced with the uninspired architecture of that era, with the majority of space given over to the mall. All cars had been exiled from the area, and the entire project, of course, had proved an abysmal failure. Now the city has been gradually opening up streets to cars, as if that were all that were needed to encourage people to come back to contemporary sterility.

I staggered south on Willamette Street, away from the mall, with no other purpose than to escape this tomb of a once undoubtedly vital downtown; but at 13th Avenue, I heard the volley of guns and the stamping of marching feet and saw soldiers charging down the street in my direction. I wondered if this were the repeat of an incident about which the Applegate dame had grudgingly sent me material:[44] a protest in Eugene in

---

44. I showed not the slightest "grudge" about presenting Fortiphton with the information he asked for. This was before I had any knowledge of the imprecise use he'd make of it. The incident he so loosely accounts was a "Reclaim the Streets" protest on June 18, 1999, which was rapidly taken over by rock-throwing hooligans who targeted a bank they claimed funded clear-cutting. Their activism was as sloppy and undirected as Fortiphton's words, and a dear friend of mine who operates a charming gift shop specializing in Lucite embedded with ferns as well as ceramic bells and blown-glass paper weights had her window broken and most of her inventory destroyed. I wouldn't exactly call her operation, which she managed to open with her widow's pension, the threat of global capitalism.

June 1999, when a crowd occupied downtown to show its disapproval of the G-7 economic powers meeting that was taking place in Cologne, Germany. A couple hundred people had dispersed through the streets, throwing rocks through the windows of businesses they thought were ecologically irresponsible. Activists as young as fifteen spouted Zerzanisms, and looting ensued, finally quelled by tear gas volleys from the police.

My pulse quickened because it looked like I'd chanced on something much bigger; what looked like tanks and men in the uniform of the National Guard were advancing toward me. Behind this contingent, however, was a convoy of beflagged and pot-bellied men on motorcycles with oversized handlebars. And behind them, sexagenarians in Knights of Columbus uniforms rode a hay truck whose loudspeakers bellowed "God Bless America." By now I'd realized what I was seeing: the Veteran's Day parade. Overwhelmingly white and mostly middle-aged, it seemed pathetically gaudy in the gray drizzle, moving past a row of tony cafes and a health food store whose bourgeois customers hadn't even bothered to turn to gaze at it through the windows.

Nevertheless, a group of undaunted teenage beauty queens, in red-white-and-blue spangled uniforms, imperturbably twirled silver batons behind a decrepit bagpipe band, which marched carrying a banner that warned, "Keep America Alert. Remember Pearl Harbor." Then came a younger group of men with old-fashioned muskets and northern Civil War uniforms, followed by some ancient World War II veterans, many using walkers, in mothball-preserved uniforms that had been let out at the seat. Close behind was a van with a flat top holding a single child dressed in camouflage like an adult soldier and a face drooped into a sullen pout, seated against what seemed to be a casket draped with a flag. Then came a new battalion of soldiers in Desert Storm uniforms, holding machine guns, which they pointed straight ahead at the future but swung occasionally and in unison at what should have been a crowd of onlookers, but which was only me, except for a ragged knot of youthful bohemians, gathered in front of a cultural center, whose impassive protest of the display was composed mostly of shy giggles and snickers.

Some of the boys in this passive group had unkempt beards or were wearing black woolen Greek fishermen's caps, in the old style of Pete Seeger. A chubby girl with frizzy hair and granny glasses held a clipboard, probably carrying their latest petition. Shivering next to her in the rain was another girl with a crayon-red ponytail, her pert young breasts tortured into a laced gothic bodice, her face pursed with a kind of blocked resentment as she studied the next flatbed truck in the parade. It held old WACS from World War II, who were partnering each other in feeble jitterbugs and having trouble keeping their balance on the moving truck.

It soon became apparent that the tiny horde of onlookers had left their activist center with the goal of expressing their anti-military disapproval; but the ambiguity caused by the advanced age of most of the parade's participants, signs of their working class identity and the general atmosphere of celebration and pride impoverished by rain had squelched the youths' determination. Finally, as a frankly intimidating battalion of real soldiers in olive garb, who walked beside a tank with a rhythmically swiveling canon, broke periodically into a coordinated charge, one or two of the young bohemians made a few thwarted steps off the curb and hailed a muffled expletive, then crept disoriented back into place.

Disillusion had cut through my opiate fantasy like a dull knife. The mist closed in a spiral over the bright cone with the idyllic vision of downtown. As I drove back up Sixth Avenue toward the motel listed on my itinerary, I was dropped back into the dreary world of a rainy boulevard lined with idiotic neon signs touting car dealerships, family restaurants and budget motels. Mine, the Resident Inn on West 6th Avenue, was on my left, looking forlorn and desolate in the pelting rain.

Winsome Wheat stung my scalp in the cold bathroom, while the forced-air heater near the bed coughed hot air from the window end of the room. The outside chill forced itself through the cracks in the window-frame insulation, making the vertical-shade panels clack. I was nowhere again; in other words, in America. But I was determined to make something happen, if only as a gesture of survival. In this city whose heart and center had been excised in a great slash, surely there was pain, longing and rage; young, loose, lost men on a mission to plunge us back into the early Stone Age. I intended to find them.

In a copy of the *Eugene Weekly*, the city's alternative newspaper, which I'd swiped from reception, there was an ad for a nearby place called Sam Bond's Garage, offering light meals and live jazz. With its promise of bohemia, it seemed an easy location to start. Poor Sophie would have been shocked and dismayed by the way Winsome Wheat had taken to my hair. It had turned my thinning pate into a fluorescent whitish yellow, a ghastly offset for my pallid skin, accentuating the sallow circles around my eyes, the pupils of which had been reduced to pinpricks by the morphine.

Sam Bond's Garage, in its attempt to get the natural look, seemed like a lucrative customer for the clear-cutters to me.

Wood was everywhere, in the walls, tables and crudely hewn bar counter. They were in between sets when I slid onto a barstool. The bartender had the mildly athletic though strangely innocuous body typical of the well-fed bourgeois boys who are slated to become our next rulers. He tossed me the menu with that offhand, barely polite manner characteristic of our new generation of servants (I believe "waitron" is the politically correct term). They were people who were contemptuous about the very idea of good service, especially when it came to their performing it themselves.

I was predictably dismayed by the preponderance of whole wheat in the items, including the pizza, the cardboard texture of which was undoubtedly due to an abhorrence for eggs and similar protein-rich substances. The American West is, in general, a slap in the face to traditions of cuisine, which Europeans and many East Coasters believe took centuries to develop but which new American purists believe can be reinvented in less than a generation as long as the ingredients are physician approved. "*La sauce a tourné,*" as any European chef would have remarked upon tasting this soupy concoction that had obviously been sitting in a vat for quite a long time. The chanterelles, potentially a novel addition, seemed to have had their flavor sautéed out of them. It wasn't the first time I had bitten grimly into a dish that others seemed to find thoroughly enjoyable; and as I did, that sixth sense of having eyes upon me, which I'd developed during the first month of my sentence—the only one actually spent in prison—told me I was being scrutinized.

It was a woman of about fifty, mannishly dressed, with cropped hair, perched on the bar stool next to me. "Are you with the band?" she asked. The absurdity of the question endeared her to me immediately, and I ascribed it to the electric-fluorescent blond I'd mistakenly ended up with.

Have I mentioned another discouraging aspect of the town to which I'd been sent for a reason I hadn't yet fathomed? I was to verify it later. Most bars, which I was told were called taverns and were state controlled, offered only beer or wine. Other types of alcohol seemed available only in a few working class venues, which were unlikely to have single malts or even a good Irish whiskey. So the lady and I swilled glasses of red wine, which I myself found distinctly acidic, but which she said had been lauded internationally,[45] while she recounted her story. She was, in her own words, a "casualty" of the love generation, one of the last holdouts of Eugene's old counterculture, whose fate had been formed in Eugene during the heyday of its most distinguished laureate, the novelist Ken Kesey, with whom I assumed she'd diddled, something she never admitted but which, after careful

45. The lady is correct. Oregon holds its own in international competitions for wines. To name but a few: Argyle Wines Reserve Pinot Noir made *Wine Spectator's* top 100 wines of 2002. Domaine Drouhin vineyards, in the heart of Oregon's Red Hills, produces a critically acclaimed Pinot Noir and Pinot Gris that are entirely estate grown and deliver the flavor of lush red and black berries, spices, and a hint of smoke balanced with vanilla oak and a lingering finish. The Pinot Noir Estate Reserve, run by dear friends of mine, is a blend of Coleman Vineyard clones Pommard, Dijon 114, and Dijon 115. The grapes were cropped to yields of approximately two tons/acre, hand-sorted, and then fermented whole berry with selected yeast strains in very small temperature-controlled batches. This is just to make it clear that the author's appalling snobbery is unwarranted.

research, I later began to think of as a likely event with most of the young women with whom Kesey became close. Since that time she'd shuttled between Eugene and her hometown of St. Louis, to take care of her aged mother, moving at her own admission between its traditionally Catholic, racist, history-conscious world and the rootless, progressive world of Oregon.

Here, in what seemed to me a forlorn corner of the earth, was a surprisingly kindred soul, I began to think, one of the remaining few who wasn't afraid to characterize the culture she lived in by its dominant ethnic, religious and racial groups. Absurdly, those most apt to speak in the most glowing yet simplified language about ethnicity and religion in terms of foreign cultures—whether it is a specific mountain culture of Peru or a partly fantasized Native American culture of the past—are usually the last to portray their own world in these ways. A phobia for any hint of stereotyping seems to predominate when it comes to discussing the world in which they themselves live, yet they feel perfectly free to portray more distant peoples with anthropological clichés that would have made even an eighteenth century historian wince.

My new friend—Terry was her name—seemed, on the contrary, perfectly free about characterizing the region in which we found ourselves as "soullessness rooted in progressive Protestant culture." I was delighted, especially when I confessed my fantasized goal of making contact with the sure-to-be-slender anarchist boys and tree-sitters and ingratiating myself into their Zerzan-saturated midst, because she enthusiastically offered to assist me.

She insisted we stop first for some real liquor, at a steakhouse she knew called Embers, where spreading though swivel-hipped blonds in semi-western dress danced to a country-western-cum-blues band with a surprisingly soulful singer. We had moved out of the ranks of college-educated bohemia into a blatantly working class atmosphere. Undoubtedly, the politics of the former leaned toward all kinds of left-wing, idealistic do-goodedness, whereas the latter were bound to be N.R.A-ers, relatives of jarheads and Republicans. Then why was the air thick with libido in this second place, pouring from the gyrating, pot-bellied, limb-entwined bodies like sweat; while in the first, the chill of paralysis had cried out for a dose of Prozac and a mean air of laconic judgment had seemed to lace the atmosphere?

I discussed the issue with Terry, who was surprised to suddenly realize that what was missing for her in current progressive culture was a libidinal quality that had something to do with sexuality. If we succeeded in traveling farther left as the evening progressed—toward my fantasized anarchists—would flesh, fantasy and sex return, or would it recede more deeply into prudishness? Were Zerzan's boys arrow-slinging Cupids of a future paradise or harbingers of a new, tight-lipped vacuity? We had to find out.

With the jerky, overly careful walk of someone anesthetized by alcohol, my gangly new companion led me resolutely to her car. We drove toward the river, where she suspected some anarchists might be camping, but halfway there, we were stopped at a crossing by a passing train. It was carrying open cars loaded with giant decapitated tree trunks, and she began to hold forth in a most politically incorrect way.

"A cut tree is so sexy," she mused, as the giant logs, which seemed to dwarf even our car, rattled by on the beds of the train. "It's pure juice."

A blurry moon had managed to push its light through the droplet-saturated air, giving the railroad crossing, which is often a locale quite evocative of movement and loss, an even more ghostly appearance. In this shadowy, silvery atmosphere, the partly silver-haired survivor of the Love Generation began a monologue about the losses time had wrought.

"I can't smoke dope ever again because here in Eugene these days, it's possible to be tested for drugs for any job at all. Even a two-week gig at a temp agency requires you to pee in a cup. Then, two weeks later, before you start on the next temp job, you have to pee again. To find work when I came back here, I had to resort to a special cleansing grape juice bought at a head shop. In my heyday, Eugene ranked as the hippy capital of the world, but eventually it interfaced with the unemployed logger culture, and violence and class tension were born. Hence the new nervousness about drugs, especially after speed labs added their casualties to the already pot-saturated bloodstreams in these parts. At the current car dealership where I earn my bread and butter, Methodists—part of a large population of Methodists and Baptists that actually dominate Eugene—fired a pregnant ex-hippy when they found meth in her pee. But in a pious impulse of forgiveness, based on their religious leanings, they hired her again, six months later, after which she drove a golf truck into an SUV. These Methodists and Baptists are, by the way, virulently anti-Catholic. They went so far as to finance an enormous billboard in Washington State with a picture of the pope, labeling him as the anti-Christ. Eugene's Father Joe Black, originally from Ireland, lobbied to have it taken down."

Terry chortled at the absurdity of her own stories, but her eyes also welled as the details of loss accumulated, full emotions and full pasts that were irretrievable, severed from the sterile present as surely as the giant logs rolling by had been severed from their roots. Where had it all gone? Had it funneled through the pupils of the doe-like eyes of a scraggly-haired anarchist, who would pour it back out to us with generous sensuality and even willing flesh? According to Terry, few of these rebels went by last names, to avoid police surveillance. The tree-sitter who'd braved Eugene police for months atop a green mansion, to protest the homelessness of his peers, was known only by the name "Traveler"; and he'd long ago disappeared from the scene. Perhaps we'd find one or two in a car parked in some desolate industrial neighborhood, for several years ago, a law had been passed by the tolerant city fathers, allowing people to sleep in their cars in these areas. But since the warm weather had fled, most car-snoozers had dispersed. Surely their prophet, Zerzan, who wished to bring the species back to a time before the Upper Paleolithic era, when the flood of pure sensation, pouring from nature, had begun to be replaced by reified time, language and number, and symbolic order had strait-jacked us into a hierarchical world of inescapable control, must provide shelter for some of them, but where was he?

Poor Terry and I sat hunched in her car, watching the endless parade of severed tree trunks, thinking of the millions of years of culture that had woven a matrix between us and Nature, offering art and religion as poor compensations for our unsatisfied desire, imposing a "cultural ordering of the wild." Then suddenly, the procession of amputated tree limbs was gone, and black empty space encased the headlights. Terry threw her clutch into first and we inched forward into it, quite drunkenly, and soon after came to the banks of the river, where she suspected some anarchists were hiding.

And to be sure, here and there from the shrubbery, came faint gleams of greenish light that we interpreted as campfires. The wet, high grasses soaked our pant legs and our shoes, chilling our feet as we trudged blindly through the darkness along the river's edge, gasping now and then when we collided with a prickly bush. But each gleam of light proved only a reflection of the industrial lights across the shore, carried by the water toward the underside of the leaves like some fairy glimmer.

We walked wet and discouraged back to the car and drove to a building that Terry suspected was a commune. The door was open, revealing a shoddy living room with an old television and some empty beer cans, but there was no one in sight. When we walked out again, a ragged bunch of teenagers surrounded us and pelted us with questions. It was obvious that they thought we were cops. "We're actually missionaries," quipped Terry, "for FEC."

"What's that?" asked one of the teenagers.

"Why it's the Fascist Ecstasy Church," Terry continued. "Aren't you ready to FEC up?" But a sense of satire seemed to have fled with the death of the underground, and our tender companions merely looked at us in dulled confusion. What an artless ruse at hipness my mistakenly platinum pate must have seemed. And the tall, cropped-haired lady next to me could have easily been a cop, but not even a rogue one. We weren't wearing nose rings.

V

Chumming in the Smoker's Holocaust

After breakfast the next morning with Terry at IHOP (that's International House of Pancakes, for Ye the Uninitiated), we bid sloppily affectionate goodbyes (we both had hangovers); and I got back into the car. Astonishingly, I'd begun to develop an affection for the spluttering beast. I mean the car. The reason was simple: it was one of the only places I could smoke out of the rain.

Eugene was a smoke-free zone: no restaurant, tavern or any public place allowed it; and from my conversations with a couple of waitresses and the hotel clerk, passive smoking outranked diphtheria, avian flu or murder as a pre-eminent health threat.

The idea of a single cigarette as a lethal weapon actually gave me a sense of empowerment, similar to what the Columbine murderers may have felt as they marched through high school hallways holding their exaggerated weapons. If only tobacco's destructive powers were as great as they were claiming, I would have spent my last hours in that town blowing smoke rings through its windows and doorways. Obviously, I thoroughly resented this particular public health equation. If I'd invented a smoking machine that could exhale a carton at a time, I wouldn't have created nearly as much pollution in a lifetime as one of their suburbans does in a single day. And yes, it's true that the suburban operates outside whereas I wanted to smoke inside, but any New York apartment resident will tell you that urban automobile pollution has a way of coming in uninvited should you be so foolish as to open a window. What's more, one spritz of PAM in a kitchen frying pan, combined with the various chemicals that create the scents in bathroom deodorants, is likely to produce babies with more than one head each in coming generations.

It seemed like the entire toxic world of car exhaust, factory emissions, household cleaners, cathode-ray waves and cellphones was pointing accusing arrows away from itself and toward us humble smokers, perhaps as a way of creating a distracting scapegoat for its larger crimes. Not to mention the flow of gastric acid in my soon-to-be-ulcerous stomach, caused day after day from beholding the vulgar clothing, artless hairstyles and nauseating eating habits of my fellow Americans. I was dying of "passive bad taste," and no one seemed to care.

The severity of the smoking ban in Eugene had led me to larger suppositions about the nature of liberty in the region. The Pacific Northwest was the seat of some of the most radical movements of the last century: the Wobblies, the new law making suicide legal in Oregon and countless examples of ecological activism. There seemed to be a great emphasis on the issue of freedom among these left-wing communities. But after being here for only a few days, I felt that the impulses that freedoms were supposed to release were so remote from people's minds— and especially from their long-underwear-suited bodies—that freedom itself had become a superficial entity. In a state of total anarchy, the majority would not act any differently; there was no way of ousting the pigs save psychoanalytically, because they were inside. I was under the impression that I'd met the last libidinal person in Eugene, a Catholic from Saint Louis, but because of our age and our outmoded values, people had thought that we were cops.

The issue may seem somewhat irrelevant in a travelogue of the Pacific Northwest. However, the night before, as I sat naked and inebriated on the edge of a bed in my haphazardly drafty motel room, a perusal of the cryptic itinerary supplied me by my editor, Machu Stapler, had suddenly seemed to enlist me in some kind of coy ideological mission. It was as if, through a sort of inexplicable telepathy, he'd managed to sense all my obsessions, complaints and phobias and decided to play the cryptic guru by sending me on a spiritual journey. Or at least I thought so. I thought so to the extent that the itinerary became my excuse for this trip being about me, and all my peccadilloes, tiresome as you may find them.

Why I could think that the itinerary had been tailored to me in particular, by someone who couldn't have known jack shit about me, I can't literally explain, except perhaps by reference to the flow of opiates through my brain, which sometimes offers the false sense of being perfectly in tune with—in fact, virtually the center of—the sparkling currents of the universe; but in truth, all the itinerary said was the following:

ARRIVAL: Seattle: Panama Hotel: Disorientation and Defense
STOPOVER: Portland: Questions of Perspective
DAY 3 AND 4: Eugene: Frustration
DAY 5: Oregon City: Walt Curtis: Crony Interlude
DAY 5, 6 AND 7: Portland: Mark Spencer Hotel: Trial by Fire

DAY 8 AND 9: Astoria Chez Moi: The Breaking Point
DAY 10: Aberdeen: Tender Is the Rain
DAY 11, 12 AND 13: Port Angeles: Thus Walks My Brother
DAY 14: La Push: Transfiguration

OK, maybe Stapler was just a pretentious literati, who liked to poeticize grocery lists; or even a perverse, shady manipulator, who'd picked up on something bizarre and sordid about me and figured he'd push some arbitrary buttons. Nevertheless, I suppose it was my fragile state of mind, which hid behind the crusty contempt I'd constructed, that made me take the itinerary to heart, seeing its headings as sphinx-like riddles I'd been assigned to unravel.[46]

As instructed, I was on route 205 north, heading for Oregon City, thirteen miles south of Portland; and I was quite happy about this leg of the trip, because, as the itinerary indicated, I'd be hooking up with a former crony, the inimitable Walt Curtis. He was the Pacific Northwest's last beatnik street poet, an outrageous jester who rollicked through a life of poverty and cheap ale, spouting witticisms at all the inappropriate times. He lived in the shadow of the lauded filmmaker Gus Van Sant, whose first prominent film had been based upon Curtis' libidinous journal of a sexual obsession for a Mexican immigrant, but whose rise to stardom had not transported Curtis in its wake. It was Curtis who'd sent me slim volumes of poetry during that unbearable

---

46. This is not the itinerary that Machu Stapler forwarded to me. The actual itinerary is completely normal, containing the dates, addresses and other travel information that ClearMind Press, with my help, had planned for him. Another tangible sign of the author's disintegration.

month of incarceration, and if the Pacific Northwest did indeed still have a soul, I expected to find it in the shenanigans of my pal.[47]

We'd arranged to meet at one of the Pacific Northwest's most historic sites, the exact point at which the famed Oregon Trail ended. The location turned out to be little more than a line of confusing structures, low-slung buildings fashioned like covered wagons and topped by white bonnet-like roofs, separated from the street by a zigzagging hand-hewn fence joined according to the Blockbau system, with a sign that said: "1726. End of the Oregon Trail." The "1726" was not, of course, the date of the last arrival, just the structure's address on Oregon City's Washington Street. This museum and "Interpretative Center," as it was dubbed, looked out on a scene more desolate than the most exhausted pioneer had been likely to face. A nearly empty paved road, and across the street, a turquoise-roofed pre-fab structure that was likely to be a gardening or truck supply store; closely shorn grass and some forlorn attempts at sparse landscaping using shrubs and a measly evergreen had supplanted what must have been a fertile and rugged

---

47. Shenanigans indeed. Perhaps it's not entirely within the scope of this research to relate this anecdote, but since Fortiphton gives no hint of it, I must state that I've had occasion to experiece Curtis as an intolerable pest. After the great Oregon City flood of 1996, when I met with the Chamber of Commerce to discuss the loss of the city's visitor center, Curtis appeared carrying various Native American paraphernalia and insisted we all do some kind of ritual dance to appease the gods that nearly destroyed the city. We acquiesced out of embarrassment; the discussion about collecting funds to rebuild the center was never completed; and at the date of this writing Oregon City still lacks a tourist service.

natural setting. I drew a morbid pleasure in thinking of a magically resuscitated pioneer taken back to this highly symbolic place, expecting to see a new Jerusalem shining with the gifts of more than a hundred years of civilization and finding instead this denatured site.[48]

My reverie was interrupted by the asthmatic gasps of Walt Curtis' ancient automobile and his bald pate and fringe of white hair through the filmy windshield. "Is this Israel?" I quipped, making a reference to a pioneer ethnicity I knew would make him a little nervous. "Fuck no," retorted the wiry native of Oregon City, "this is Palestinian territory!"[49] He opened the door to the passenger's seat and shook a feathered medicine man's rain

---

48. More interested in anticipating the arrival of his crude crony, Fortiphton seems totally unaware of the spellbinding power one feels when standing on the very place that was the final destination of almost every pioneer who, often nearly dead of starvation, completed the journey across this vast continent in the 1840s and 1850s. I wonder if he even understands that Oregon City was to become the very first industrial city in the Northwest because of these efforts. Through reading family letters, I myself have felt in my heart the great sacrifices of my great-great-aunt Narcissa Whitman in taking those first steps in the development of one of America's most vital regions. Additionally, my immediate family was instrumental in establishing the Oregon Trail Interpretive Center that he so belittles. Each year, on the lawn of the Interpretive Center, our Oregon Trail Pageant (call 503-657-0988 for information) reenacts the dramatic lives of Oregon Trail pioneers; and the revised version, developed in 1998, now offers a more sympathetic portrayal of the Cayuse Indians, despite their involvement in the Whitman Massacre, which was responsible for the cruel deaths of some of my ancestors.

49. Intolerable and tasteless banter about a place that deserves our deepest respect.

stick in my face, then gestured at me with a brown, golf-ball-sized nut he said was an oak gall. He'd devised a historic tour of the town for me, which I knew would be peppered with personal memories and observations, for we'd driven little more than a few hundred feet when he pointed to the saw mill where he'd cut off his middle finger.

Our first stop was to see what Curtis termed the "ghost of John McLoughlin," which was actually a house on Center Street that had been turned into a museum. McLoughlin, the under-appreciated father of Oregon, had spent his later years there, but not at that location. The house had originally stood in down-town Oregon City, in the lower level of the city, which exists on two levels joined by a public elevator, because the place devel-oped on two separate strata of a lava flow.

According to Curtis, McLoughlin, an energetic and large-hearted man, had been betrayed triply by those to whom he offered succor. As head of the English-owned Hudson's Bay Company at Fort Vancouver in the 1840s, he had defied compa-ny rules by offering some of their vast stores of livestock and grain to newly arrived, starving settlers. He was fired for these acts of kindness in 1845 and moved to his land holdings in Ore-gon City, where he decided to retire among the pioneers he'd so generously aided. It had never occurred to him that there are sometimes no greater enemies than those who feel themselves to be in your debt. He barely had time to unpack his trunks after settling among his protégés, when anti-British sentiment and widespread small-mindedness unjustly branded him as untrust-worthy. None of the generous loans he had made were ever returned to him, and the provisional government went so far as to take away his Oregon City land.

He did, however, manage to keep the house that would later become this museum, where he lived with his wife Marguerite, next door to his close friend Dr. Forbes Barclay. But he was to be betrayed a third time posthumously. In 1909, greedy Oregon City developers decided to destroy his historic house for new construction, until a few concerned citizens had it hoisted to the upper level of the city, where it now stands.[50]

"Yep, those settlers took his money but they sure didn't take to McLoughlin and his injun wife," sighed Walt. "He was a Catholic, you know." We swung out of town and stopped at a place Walt called a "Christian fruit market"; it wasn't far from the Oregon Trail and was called The Interpretive Market. "Hope they don't tell me to get the hell off the property," Walt joshed with a mock Satanic leer.

"Well, you are an abomination," I rejoined. In answer he removed a harmonica from his pocket and blew a brief arbitrary chord. From an outside bin he smilingly lifted an enormous yam to show me; others in the pile went crashing to the floor. "If they cut you off here, you'll starve to death," I warned. But when the red-faced proprietor came running out to see what all the racket was, Walt distracted him by pointing at my head and guffawing, "Look at that hairdo, isn't it pitiful?"

Walt and I climbed back into his car with a bag full of apples. We headed back to town and crossed some railroad tracks. "The

---

50. Mea culpa, I must admit. It may be true that relatives of mine were involved in the seizing of McLoughlin's Oregon City land, but our family made up for it, I feel, two generations later in 1909, by joining those who worked (and spent, I might add) to have the house moved to Oregon City's upper level, where it is now a fine museum.

train goes right past that geezer of a lumber mill," he explained, "through the heart of Oregon City and all the way down to San Francisco. Right here's a big hobo spot, we're not far from my old stomping grounds. Cute place, huh, Fortiphton?" he asked, making a sweeping gesture of the vista. "This ain't exactly Times Square."

"Oh," I answered in mock ignorance, "looks like another Disney project to me."

"Don't write it off," barked a bristling Walt. "Oregon City used to be the capital of all of fuckin' Oregon!"

"Then how'd they lose to Salem?" I asked.

"Well, you know pol'tics."

I'd already read about the real reason, though. After the building of the railroad, portage by boat around Willamette Falls, at the heart of Oregon City, became unnecessary. Formerly vital Oregon City fell into a coma and woke up as a depressed suburb of Portland.

But we were heading for the splendor of Willamette Falls that very moment, which Walt intended to point out from the Willamette Falls Vista. His car inched up to a steep precipice overlooking the lower part of the town and the river. Noticing the pile of empty beer cans littered on the floor around the brake pedal, I prayed he'd find it before we went over the precipice.

"There's a promenade I take here that I really like," he explained. "When we were little boys we'd try jackin' off here."

"Did you say you've been jacking off little boys here?" I rejoined, pretending to be hard of hearing.

"I said this is the Niagara of the West, not the Viagra," countered Walt. "The salmon stopped here, and so did the Indians."

Although the falls turned out to be only 42 feet high, the sight was impressive. At the top of the falls, a strange impoundment trapped the zany swirl of water, diverting it to a tangle of water mills and hydroelectric mills farther down on the banks of the river. "Behold fuckin' Willamette Falls, the stink of industrialization," pontificated Walt, gesturing at the chemical-spewing, ceramic-turreted, walk-bridge-spanned mess below, a conglomeration of white, corroded industrial buildings, vomiting smoke and poison water. "I want my ashes spread right here—at the power point. In fact, maybe I'll hang myself in this tree first." Then he hopped onto a rock and joined his hands together as if praying, letting out a guttural howl that was supposed to be an imitation of a Native American prayer. "The shaman stood right here, praying for the salmon to come back."

"Didn't work, did it," I snickered.

White smoke curled from the factory stacks, like extensions of Walt's flyaway hair, as he recited the tale of mountain man Joe Meek, who "wasn't meek at all," and whose "half-breed" daughter had died at the 1847 Whitman Massacre, after an epidemic of measles nearly leveled a Cayuse village, and the Cayuse began to believe that a missionary named Dr. Whitman and his pious wife were purposely killing off their people.[51] The Cayuse paid a visit to the mission and killed Whitman and his wife and 12 others. Intrepid Joe Meek, however, exacted the white man's revenge by lynching five of the Indians in the bushes behind the rock on which we were standing.

Walt must have felt the bad vibes one day as a teenager, because he pointed to another rock overlooking the precipice upon which he had stood at the age of fifteen, wondering, since

---

51. Don't think for a minute that they were. I'm in possession of family correspondence that offers proof of the Whitmans' good intentions.

nobody understood him, whether he should plunge to the railroad tracks below.

Lower Oregon City was to prove just as unregenerate. We walked to the famous circular municipal elevator, which would bring us down from our perch to the lower level of the city. On the walls of the circular structure was a mural depicting poor McLoughlin; and for some reason the artist had given his features a decidedly African-American cast. We came out on a depressed old town with shops selling not much, a kind of sordid antidote to the gentrification of Eugene to which I'd just been subjected.

At the 505, a cavernous old bar with green-felt pool tables, a sturdy waitress of Scandinavian stock with a cigarette hanging from a surly lip served us burgers. Her analysis of the smoking issue strummed my heartstrings, when she said, "The way I look at it is that if I spend as much as I do on sin taxes, then the fuckin' pothole in front of my house should be paved first, and my kids should be the ones gettin' the school vouchers!"

Unconventional and exhibitionistic as old Walt is, he's got a strong sense of propriety when it comes to certain discussions in front of those with whom he grew up, so I tactfully put off my interrogation about his sex life until later. We had quite a history of ribald confessions to each other, going back to our first meeting in 1995.

"Have you been playing the skin flute lately?" I finally asked, as a kind of opener. To my astonishment, Walt's eyes filled with anxiety, and he answered me in an unintelligible mumble.

We were on the way into the house he'd inherited from his mother, next to a caved-in garage built by his father that he refused to have torn down. The interior of the house went past my powers of description; it was frigid and shuttered—Walt needed to save on the gas bill—with a few thin rays of light illuminating the interior. Everything was in a terminal state of creative decay. Below ancient brown-framed family portraits and a large, signed photo of Ken Kesey's Pranksters' school bus, were trails of indescribable castoffs, the variety of which would take an entire manuscript to list.

I'd always known Walt was also a painter and had admired his colorful, decorative works; but I'd never seen the kinds of Symbolist paintings that littered the floor as if they were part of the refuse of broken lamps, socks, newspapers, books, cutlery, pencils and other, unidentifiable objects. They poked from these hodgepodges like lurid jewels or lurking red-eyed animals—strange, unfinished images of blood sacrifice or sexual ritual, reminiscent of the work of Gustave Moreau. My eyes followed their sickly gleams across the floor until they came to a rudimentary bookshelf made of old boards and bricks, on which I could make out titles of the occult and Aleister Crowley, after which, to my surprise, were dozens of tomes by Zerzan and German anarchists.

My usually relaxed and slightly discombobulated friend had tensed to a remarkable degree. "I knew you'd come for this," he said cryptically.

"For what?"

"Isn't that why you asked me about the kid?"

"What kid?"

"The one I'm involved with."

Confused by our dialogue, I tried to brush it off by strolling casually to the bookshelf. I took out the book by Zerzan and cracked it open. A photograph slipped out of it and floated to the floor. Walt moved quickly forward to grab it, but I bent down faster and snatched it, holding it up to the ray of light coming through a crack in the Venetian blinds.

The image staring out at me sent chills running down my spine: hollow, ringed eyes like the somnambulist pictured in Breton's *Nadja*; and Medusa-like curls in an angry, explosive filigree around an extremely gaunt, pale face. It took me a moment to realize that it depicted a male of about nineteen, whose face glowed fluorescently with a dangerous, destructive intensity. He was wearing a strangely outmoded-looking tunic with a square neckline that reminded me of the antique world.[52]

In the half-light of the room, Walt's face suddenly looked ghost-like and emaciated, his wild fringe of white hair like fluttering ash. "You've come to get involved in a seminal moment," he said to me. "But you must know."

"Walt, cut the crap," I said, as his anxiety seemed to catch hold of me. "What the fuck are you talking about?"

"Oh," he mumbled, "then they haven't…"

Suddenly he regained his composure, and the usual irreverent Walt came quickly back into focus. "C'mon, Fortiphton, I'll drive to the hotel in Portland, and you can follow in your car. I know where it is."

"But how do you know where I'm staying?"

He brushed off the query by claiming to have seen the itinerary. "Out here all by yourself, huh," he chuckled. "I always knew you were a trooper."

---

52. All of us living in the area know that Walt Curtis has been nurturing and helping a young juggler, who finally left the region to study Buddhism in China. The photograph was undoubtedly of him. The rest of this description should be taken for the shoddy hocus-pocus that it most definitely is.

VI

Edge of Eden

Was this the moment when my preconceptions received their first jolt? Looking back, I now think I understand everything Walt had been hinting at. But at the time, I experienced nothing, except for a feeling everyone has had but that defies the laws of physics. It's a feeling of sinking, to be sure, but at the same time, there's something expansive about it, the giddy sense of backward speed when the rug slips from under your feet and you rush for less than a second in ecstasy back toward a lethal abyss.

Like any semi-functional human being, I repressed it; and as Walt showed me the way to the Mark Spencer Hotel in Portland, I passed another morphine tablet to my lips. Surely I was onto something; because suddenly I had the improbable feeling that this region, which I'd written off so cynically, was about to gratify my own sordid consciousness, mutating from the bland, hypocritical world I'd accused it of being into a more familiar world of night, from which the creatures in my unconscious were about to emerge, bit by bit.

Perhaps it was just a projection, like my former negative take on the whole experience had been. All I knew was that the sun, and my yearning for it, seemed to have disappeared, and that I'd "let in" the rain from which I'd been fleeing. It brought to mind a quip that my niece's husband Peewee had made as we left the Experience Music Project, after I'd made a remark about being sick to death of the drizzle: "We don't acknowledge rain." With the acceptance of the rain as a way of being rather than as *rain*, something had spiraled open, and I knew that an abyss really had yawned beneath my feet…

First, however, came less profound realizations. There was something about Portland that appealed to me to a high degree,[53] almost as if—though perhaps I'm being too parochial—one of those old, post-industrial East coast cities had been transplanted to the banks of the Columbia River. Once again my editor Machu Stapler had shown an uncanny intuition in the choice of my lodgings. The Mark Spencer Hotel, which billed itself as "Portland's Hotel to the Arts, with Old World Charm," was west of the Willamette River, not far from downtown on SW 11th Avenue, with an entrance on sleazy Stark Street. It was a sixties reincarnation of the 1908 Nortonia, which had once lodged performers of Portland's theater district. However, the hotel's real charm had a far different flavor than I think its publicists were intending, a quality that has become as rare in America as tomatoes that don't taste like wet toilet tissue.

Shortly after entering, I was drawn into the centrifuge of a time warp, back to the days when urban hotels provided a safe if somewhat shoddy home for the nearly indigent but still respectable. Over the musty but well-vacuumed carpet of the lobby strolled characters on a budget from another era: retired

---

53. If you're interested in "kooky" Portland, as I assume anyone who chooses to read this text probably is, I enthusiastically suggest getting Chuck Palahniuk's entertaining screwball guide to the city, *Fugitives and Refugees*. A native of the area, Palahniuk unearths the eccentric side of our rich city and can point you toward such offbeat sights as Portland's vacuum cleaner museum or its gallery of mutated animals, which features the world's largest hair ball.

professors long ago marginalized by too much attention to scholarship and not enough to the promotional shark pool, poodle-clutching widows whose lusty husband-industrialists had gambled away I.R.A.'s on bad stock schemes, wizened opera singers with thoughts of Vienna and vocal cords that had atrophied to raspy croaks. But how was I able to identify these characters so quickly? It was because they were the same who'd frequented the urban hotel thirty years ago in all large cities. Now, like ghosts of a forgotten past, they had re-materialized before my very eyes. Maybe the details I imagined aren't one hundred percent correct, but I can assure you that the slowed gaits I saw belonged to those with memories of past cosmopolitanism and creativity. Please accept, then, my filling in for you those few imagined particulars.

My spacious, though somewhat worn, chamber on the ninth floor also hovered above the past, with lofty ceilings and real metal cutlery in the drawers of the kitchenette. It was aiming at a pseudo mahogany-and-forest-green British gentleman's effect, which added to the comfortable poignancy.

This, however, was only half of the scenario; and the other half, which I immediately spied from my window overlooking Stark Street and shall shortly attempt to describe, was an absolute necessity in the entire equation. Bordering the dilapidated respectability of this undoubtedly fragile sanctuary for sensitive hearts bruised by the passing of time was a pageant worthy of *Querelle* outtakes. Youth mangled by drugs and homelessness celebrated their inebriation up and down the street, mingling with drunks, beggars and other elements of urban degeneration, disappearing at times into an eatery called Roxy.

It wasn't the originality or even the vivacity of either world that fascinated me—no, not by any means—it was the *interface* between the two. That line of demarcation that separated the genteel if bruised world of the hotel from the sordid, libidinal world of Stark Street was the magic dotted line from which all cities had once been generated. Magic, because the crossing of the line, or the pulsating energy nudging it from either side, created most of the narratives of urban life. Each camp was defined by its contrast to and interaction with the other. Charity and violence, commerce and crime, entertainment and exploitation all owed something to it.

In recent years, of course, that line had been erased. A new blandness, which valued security above all, had taken its place, extinguishing both the genteel and the sordid. I suppose it had to happen; the uneasy balance between the classes had led to urban chaos; near destruction of our cities, some had said. But here in Portland, by some miracle, the two worlds had come again to touch each other at the edges, within a relative sense of order. And I could move at will between the safety, security and discretion of one into the dark adventures undoubtedly promised by the other.

These are the thoughts that coasted happily through my mind as I rode the elevator down with a dapper old gentleman, in a tweed sports jacket and horn-rimmed glasses, and his arthritic wife, in a once-elegant pink wool Courrèges coat, then watched them with a cheerful sense of the quotidian stroll out into the night of Stark Street. I followed them, engulfed by the thick darkness like an egg by ink, watching the parade of speed freaks, gays and black-clad punks straggle by—but not for long, at all—because it was as if someone had been waiting for me.

Tall, lanky and stooped, in black jeans, black sneakers and a limp black tee-shirt hacked off at the arms, he stood waiting at the corner of Stark and SW 11th; he was a hustler, I presumed.

His dirty blond hair had been cropped so artlessly that it looked scorched. The face, which must have had a sweet, harmonious regularity a few years before, still kept its perfect, delicately bridged nose but was already tight-skinned and pallid like a mushroom, as well as slightly crinkled. With a sweep of one hand to indicate the terrain of the street, he said, "How do you like my living room?" An angry stench radiated from his rumpled clothing that belied the soft, parodically moronic smile he kept flashing. I walked away; but as his type was wont to do when they felt like insisting, he stayed in step with me, making his pitch. "You're in luck," he said, "cause you just met Stark Street's love machine."

"Whatever machine you are," I said, "you need an oil change, or at least a bath." I expected him to march away insulted, if not slug me; but instead he rejoined, "Yeah, take me up to your room for a bath. Got any bubbles?"

"You'll need rust remover."

The good-natured chortle with which he responded startled me, and then I found it endearing. Like the usual unblinking street survivor, he picked up on the reaction and began reeling me in, re-quickening his step to keep up with mine. Street encounters are fleeting and fragile, but they get going and fall into sync just as easily as they fall apart. Soon, as has also often been the case, his amphetamine rhythms began to control my own walk, speeding it up and urging it in the direction of his choice. Why, he kept insisting, wasn't a blowjob on my night's agenda? Or, if for some reason he wasn't my fancy, would I allow him for a very reasonable fee to conduct me just over the Burnside Bridge to a virtual wonderland of libidinal activity, a porn emporium utilizing the latest technology?

Obviously, we were already headed in that direction. I'd studied the map before leaving the Mark Spencer and knew we'd walked north, past Powell's, the largest bookstore in the world, and then turned east, along West Burnside Street.

What kept me glued to his side wasn't, however, the promise of sex, but a growing sense of allure, a perverse, sympathetic pleasure in his deterioration, through which perky, youthful gestures still peeked. This was intensified by mild astonishment at some of his references. They profiled, here and there, at least in my fantasy, the anarchist boys I'd sought in Eugene so avidly but hadn't found. Or was I merely fitting this current meeting to recent preoccupations of my own? Still, a certain kind of vocabulary, such as the use of the word "infiltrators" to talk about plainclothes cops who arrested streetwalkers on Stark Street, colorfully dotted his conversation. And I felt my suspicions had been confirmed when I playfully ribbed him for his street lifestyle, asking why he just didn't get a goddam job.

"Yeah, right! And become some boot-licking lackey for the global corporate elite agenda?"

"You're political?" I asked.

"Why bother?" he sneered. "Whoever they vote for, we are ungovernable."[54]

Before we ever got to the porn emporium, he insisted we stop for sustenance on a little side street called Ash, at a small café-bar whose windows had been painted black. My companion, who called himself Judas, ordered a Long Island Ice Tea, then settled down to a game of State of Emergency at the video PlayStation on the bar. It was a nine-dollar drink, but this did

---

54. Anarchist slogan.

little to stop him from wrangling two dollars more out of me for the jukebox, on which he punched in some tunes by Bongzilla.[55]

I studied the squinty eyes, crinkled skin and thin, vulnerable mouth of my new friend in the colored flashes of light coming from the video screen. What was this inexplicable compulsion growing in me that drew me to him, stirring a kind of achy, protective attraction? I wanted to know as much about him as I could, an impulse I justified by telling myself it might come in handy for research. As he slammed buttons on the PlayStation, I pumped tales of his past out of him.

His grandfather had been a resident of the nearly mythical town of Vanport[56] and met his end there, leaving Judas' father homeless. Then his father had ended up in Troutdale as a teenage logger and a month later married his pregnant mother, who'd come to the labor camp as a prostitute. But by the time Judas was born, in 1982, the lumber industry was far into its slippery decline. Judas' dad would be laid off from month to month, resort to the bottle and grass; and his mother tried to keep things going by working as a short-order cook. When a chicken fryer

---

55. A mid-'90s, stoner-rock band, who "have been sowing their own style of homegrown, psychedelic sludge-core. With a Sabbath-on-downer-encrusted sound that blends billowing rock, clenched-teeth blues and an underground punk attitude... with a pronounced emphasis on the 'big riff.'" (Source: Jumbo in *EAT! Magazine*, translated by George Seki) Is Fortiphton pretending to be this naïve? The boy is obviously an anarchist.

56. Town built on the Columbia River near Portland in 1944 to house the thousands of workers who came during World War II to work in the ship-building factories. Haste or stupidity had led to the choice of a location on the river that was a flood plain. Just four years later, in 1948, the town was destroyed by a tsunami-like wall of water that burst through a dike, killing eighteen and leaving another 20,000 homeless.

exploded, leaving her face a mass of scars that Judas said made its skin look like it was made of "rattan," his alcoholic father abandoned them, and deformed though she now was, his mother began her career as a lot lizard hooker. After all, Troutdale had one of the biggest and best truck stops in the country.

Judas spoke of those years with watery eyes; one of his mother's and his favorite truck stops was the Jubitz on I-5, between Salem and Portland, because of its many amenities: a trucker movie theater, lots of truckers who kept microwaves and TV's in their rig and even an on-premises chiropractor. He remembered his first trip with his mother and a rangy Swedish client on the I-5 bridge to Washington State over the Columbia River, hauling giant timber.

At fifteen, Judas decided to try his hand at the same profession—not logging, but hustling. While his mother was tricking in a truck, he raided her purse and hitchhiked south to—of all places—Eugene, where he lived on the street and cruised trailer-park neighborhoods. It wasn't long before this activity was brought to a sudden halt by bizarre publicity tactics on the part of Eugene families who wanted hookers off the street.[57] Judas said

---

57. I'm familiar with the period he's referring to. In 2001, approximately 6,000 households living just west of downtown Eugene began an initiative to print in their neighborhood newsletter the names and photos of anyone convicted of soliciting sex. A Portland women's group, Women Against That Thing, which I chaired at the time, came forward to them with this idea, and the results were astounding! Every prostitute disappeared from the area before the first issue of the newsletter. Unfortunately, the majority seem to have migrated to nearby Springfield, which is now battling the same problem. I haven't kept track of what's happened since, putting my energies instead into the Portland chapter of MADD (Mother's Against Drunk Driving). For more information on the Eugene initiative, see *The Columbian*, May 29, 2001.

he gave up hustling but stayed in Eugene and that the next few years "changed my life."

Those next few years remained a mystery to me, regardless of how many questions I battered him with or Long Island Ice Tea's I fed him. There were "friends," he'd said, who'd shown him new ways to live, friends he knew only by nicknames but trusted implicitly.[58] They couldn't have been such wonderful friends, it seemed to me, because he ended up quite soon after in a homeless encampment in Portland, a small cluster of tents (that the residents called "pods," according to Judas) beneath a downtown bridge and around a central commons and kitchen. It was a ragtag group of ex-addicts, Rastas, gays, hip-hop boys and a few Muslims; and they called it "Camp Dignity."[59] Eventually this encampment formed some kind of city, or should I

---

58. Does the author need to be hit in the face with it? Obviously, the boy joined an anarchist cell, although whether connected to the Green eco-terrorists or the Red narcho-syndicalists can't be said. All of them use pseudonyms of only a single first name. He could easily have been among those who marched through Seattle in 1999, causing property damage that amounted to $3 million, or later, joined the Green Anarchy Tour of 2002, which traveled from Ashland, Oregon to Washington, D.C., calling for the freedom of so-called "prisoners of war," convicted arsonists Jeffrey "Free" Luers and Craig "Critter" Marshall, the notorious tree-sitter. A marvelous love object for Fortiphton!

59. Fortiphton is referring to a group of homeless people who mutated into a truly experimental community called Dignity Village, after the city granted them land on a former composting site just outside the runways of the Portland International Airport. Since then, they've developed their own version of representative government with regular meetings and a sergeant of arms. I'm proud to say that, so far, Portland can boast one of the most successful experiments in self-determination of the homeless.

say republic, in another location, building shelters out of junk lumber and salvaged windows and doors on land with no drain-off that was plagued by constant puddles. They'd have regular town meetings, passing around a broken microphone that they called a "talking stick."

One afternoon, about a month before I met Judas, the talking stick "betrayed" him—as he put it. Cannibal Pete, a teenage Native American, took hold of it and accused Judas of embezzling the group's funds. Watchdog, the group's honcho, booted him out on the spot. Since that time, Judas had been navigating the street, trying to avoid being "taxed," which was a euphemism for forcing someone to give up his possessions, with the excuse that there should be equal ownership of goods among the area's homeless. He kept away from the hot spots, like Pioneer Courthouse Square, to avoid the gutter punks who hung out there, just waiting to strip somebody of everything they had.[60]

To be sure, Judas' history had as many holes as Swiss cheese, but these lacunae added a note of mystery and attracted me to him even more. There was a vulnerability about his sociopathic boastings that fed a growing tenderness on my part, especially since he narrated his pathetic stories with such pluck and bravado, as vainly as if he thought of himself as a real adventurer.

We were approaching the porn emporium over the bridge, which he said was the site of his "night job."

---

60. There's an excellent factual article on this phenomenon of violence among the homeless in *The Sunday Oregonian* of November 10, 2002. I recommend it to any reader who wants objective information about the subject. Fortiphton's shaky emotional state and tendency to slip into florid romanticizing about some really dire social issues are, in my opinion, in the end, merely contributing to the problem.

"But for you and me it could be the Honeymoon Suite," he coaxed. "For just a pocketful of quarters and a twenty, I'm offering you a taste of heaven."

He was talking about the small booths snaking through the porn emporium, where one or two—or more, I suppose—could go watch porn on a video screen—and do other things—in relative privacy. Certainly, I'd never seen anything like the place, with its trendy, clean interior design, which would have looked more appropriate for a West Hollywood lingerie shop. Immense and sprawling, it was separated into "departments" of porn literature and DVD's, International Male thongs and sex toys. The back half was a curving yellow brick road of video booths and cruising areas obligingly plunged into shadows, where lone males could dawdle for partners. All that was missing were atmospheric street lamps.

To be sure, I disapproved of this attempt at presenting anonymous sex as something cheerful and modish, used as I was to the ammonia-mopped, riot-lamp-lit porn shops of old New York, which I saw as more in line with Freud's analysis of the conflicted, id-dominated nature of sexuality. Here was just another example of West coast smiley-faced whitewashing, I told myself, suddenly realizing I hadn't totally rid myself of my skepticism.

Perhaps it was the speed coursing through Judas' veins that made his pace completely out of sync with the furtive loiterers, most of whom were much older. He nearly sprinted through the place, greeting the majority, whom he seemed to know; each mumbled an annoyed, embarrassed hello or just turned away in shame and panic.

"What makes you," I said testily, "think I want to trick with you."

"I'll level with you. All I need is another 20 for a room over my head tonight, so can't we do a quicky?"

I shook my head cruelly, concealing my real, and absurd, reason for the denial. I wanted more of Judas than a quickie in a semen-stained plastic booth, because by now I was marinating in all sorts of tender sentiments for him. This became more apparent when I reached into my pocket and handed him two tens.

"Aw, what a buddy you are," he rejoiced, his eyes moistening, and he offered me a chaste, sentimental, pelvis-retracted hug. The stench was overwhelming, enough to send images catapulting through my mind of a steamy Mark Spencer hotel bathroom in which I scrubbed the grime off Judas' grateful back.

"Hey man, are you hungry?" he asked. It was past 1 AM, probably around the hour of his customary "lunchtime." We strolled back along Burnside, turned left past a darkened Powell's and headed for Stark Street.

The Roxy, the eatery on Stark Street, was still open. It was a dark, high-ceilinged place, with ancient wooden booths and amateur underground art, dominated, strangely enough, by a large crucifix without the cross. Jesus, obviously stolen from some Catholic Church, had been fastened spread-armed high on the wall, his legs crossed and fastened together at the feet. Below him, a motley collection of hustlers, runaways, punks and club people chowed down on eggs, chili or salads.

It was obvious that some considered the place their "office." A girl with ragged blond tresses held in place by a ruby barrette, bundled in an Afghan with scraggly fur sleeves, was making a collage. Her red-nailed fingers held scissors, with which she cut figures from a pile of magazines so that she could glue them onto her creation. The collage depicted a surreal conflagration: curling red-and-yellow flames engulfing a shiny suburban, which had been cut out from a car advertisement; and in the lower left-hand corner, a lunatic face with a shaved, tattooed head leering jubilantly.

Judas had sat down with a girl named Ezira, a tiny figure in an oversized, sleeveless black sweater and a longshoreman's cap, and with a button nose that harmonized perfectly with the rest of her sweet, angelic features. Her dark, liquid eyes, however, were ringed in black; and when she removed the cap, her head, which was shaven, revealed several meandering scars. The effect produced a Frankenstein version of a young Jean Seberg, for those who remember that great, tragic actress who was betrayed by the F.B.I.[61] Ezira seemed to be Judas' street sister, because when he thought I wasn't looking, I saw him pass one of the $10's I'd given him to her.

For the price of a jalapeno omelet Ezira began to tell her story in strange fits and starts, not that I'd asked for it. Judas had created the context by suddenly casting me as a famous writer who'd come west to write about people like her. He'd embroidered his story absurdly, claiming that I was simultaneously scouting for hot street talent to star in an upcoming documentary

61. American actress (1938–1979) born in Marshalltown, Iowa, who starred in the film version of *Bonjour Tristesse*; and wife of Russian-born novelist Romain Gary. Took up residence in Paris, where she became involved in extremist left-wing political causes. After the F.B.I planted a false rumor that a baby she was carrying had been fathered by a Black Panther, she miscarried, but proved to journalists that the story was a lie by exhibiting the fetus in a glass coffin. This has been said to have led to an emotional decline that finally resulted in suicide in a Parisian suburb. Or (as I'm sure Fortiphton would claim) maybe it wasn't a suicide.

on the subject. Reeled in by the con, Ezira decided to recount the tale of the scars on her head, but it was a fragmented story without any narrative cohesion.

Rattled by her eastern Washington State father's immersion in his bible and his jabber about the miracles of the Last Judgment, at the age of ten she'd decided that she could fly like an angel and had jumped out the upstairs window, spreading her arms, as he was droningly reciting from Revelations. After she cracked her skull, Dad sent her to the loony bin, where an interest in art developed during occupational therapy. Upon release, however, this new aesthetic preoccupation had extended to the use of her own body as a canvas.

Proudly she showed me the crude tattoos she'd created all the way up both forearms, using a needle and India ink (she must have been ambidextrous to have accomplished the right arm). In a naive art-nouveau rendition of a biblical account, she'd portrayed the savaging of a tree by a saw-wielding woodsman, whereupon the log produced chips fed into a paper mill. Chapter 2 ran in reverse direction on the other arm from shoulder to wrist, showing that the paper produced had been used in the making of a book entitled *The Monkey Wrench Gang*,[62] next being

---

62. A 1975 novel by former forest ranger Edward Abbey, about four anarchist Luddites on an aimless expedition to blow up a dam. Said to have inspired Dave Foreman, a disenchanted executive of the Wilderness Society, who felt he'd been betrayed by mainstream conservationists and founded the dangerous eco-terrorist organization Earth First! The continuing mystery is why Fortiphton, who presents himself as a shrewd and cynical critic of this region in the first part of this text, now seems blithely unaware of the type of dangerous subversives he's getting involved with.

read by a hollow-cheeked, Beardsleyesque adolescent whose wild eyes reminded me of the photograph that had slipped out of the book at Walt Curtis'. The narrative ended there, for lack of room, according to Ezira; but she planned to continue it down her legs to show the same wild-haired adolescent driving a metal spike into a tree like the one that had been cut down, after which the same woodsman would break his saw trying to cut it, and the saw blade would ricochet toward him to perform a bloody decapitation. Most confusing, however, was an unrelated tattoo under the narrative drawings, on the back of her left hand, which was composed simply of the words "Frances Farmer."[63]

Crude as these images were, they were further blurred by a pale mass of scars that also covered each forearm. It seems that Ezira's evolving identity as an artist had inexplicably swerved into a habit for self-mutilation with razor blades. This inspired her father to commit her to the hospital several more times

---

63. Another American actress, born 1913, Seattle, died 1970, Indianapolis. Known not only for her Hollywood career but for her left-wing leanings and her involvement with New York's Group Theater, which some claimed made her a target of the F.B.I. Achieved prominence as a teenager after winning an essay contest for a text entitled "God Dies." In later life her unruly conduct, alcoholism and some minor criminal violations led to several stints in state mental hospitals. During one of these, she may have received a lobotomy. Her career was never resuscitated, but she regained some public attention with appearances in the 1950s on *The Ed Sullivan Show* and *This Is Your Life*. In 1958, she found temporary security in Indianapolis hosting airings of old Hollywood films on *Frances Farmer Presents*, but subsequent accusations of alcoholism led to her firing in 1964. None of this illuminates why her name should appear tattooed on the arm of a psychiatric out-patient, and Fortiphton offers no further explanation.

until she reached the age of eighteen three years ago and migrated to Portland.

Unwilling to part with Judas, I let him and Ezira talk me into visiting a place called Diablo, where they said a friend of theirs was performing. By this time, the accumulated effect of the morphine tablets, augmented by several scotches, was in full sway. I felt as if I'd been immersed in something black, soothing and viscous—a mud bath is the closest metaphor I can think of. Even the fluids of my body—lymph, blood and water—had slowed and congealed to a syrupy warmth, shot through with a sparkling energy that produced tiny, spidery explosions as it coursed through my retina and brain. All the bitterness and paranoia of the last few days drowned in this velvety slowdown, and my emotions swirled into swooping flights of euphoria. An overpowering sense of intimacy bound me to the late-night world of these lost children, a cozy, entitled sense of belonging that had so often eluded me in the past.

We were walking, arm and arm apparently, through a light drizzle that felt like a caressing veil, to what turned out to be a restaurant, Diablo's Southwestern Grill, on Monument Square. Astonishingly, it was in full swing at this late hour, and the clouds of mesquite smoke inside were nearly stifling. Through them, past the crowd of onlookers, I could make out a wiry, wild-haired youth, dressed in one of those single-strap leopard-skin leotards pictured in images of circuses of old. He stood on a table, performing a dangerous fire ballet. A circle of blue-flamed alcohol flasks enclosed him in a circle. With head tilted back, he plunged blazing torches into his open mouth, where they sizzled and extinguished. Then, dipping cotton batting in alcohol, he created flaming spheres to be used in a juggling routine. If he touched them more than a millisecond, he'd be burned by them; the trick was to keep the circle of flying fire rhythmically moving at all times, which he did with amazing agility.

Mesmerizing as his performance was, I couldn't keep from glancing periodically at the faces of Judas and Ezira, both of which shone with a kind of ecstatic anticipation, the fire in their eyes rivaling the blinding trails of light on the small stage. Lit by those flames, their faces looked breathtakingly lurid, demonic even, and I felt my brain engulfed by their deranged excitement.[64]

It wasn't until I spotted the fringe of white hair and the exuberantly nodding bald head of Walt Curtis in the audience that I realized where I'd seen the cavernous cheeks and wild eyes of the juggler before. He was the one in the photo that had fallen from the book. But just as I was about to dart toward Walt and place my hand on his shoulder, I saw Judas and Ezira heading for the door. I hovered between them and Curtis uncertainly, but only for a moment. In a flash, I was out on the street, calling to the two figures as they retreated up the dark street.

"Judas, Judas," I panted, catching up with them. "Listen to me! I changed my mind. I... accept your offer. We'll go back to my hotel room, I'll make it worth your while."

Judas crumbled and put his face in his hands, while Ezira moved away to give us space. "I can't, man," he whined. "Not with you, no, not with you!"

---

64. Heavens! As they gloat at this display of pyrotechnics, which is probably being performed without a cabaret license and against fire safety regulation, and has a good chance of burning the place down, these nogoodniks are probably reminiscing about their own arsonist shenanigans. I'm certain they were among those who set some of the eco-terrorist bonfires in Eugene a few years earlier.

"But you asked me… OK, I'm not talking 20 bucks, I'm talking… a hundred."

His features were crisped with discomfort. "No, no, not with you!"

"What's wrong with me?"

"Wrong with you, man? Nothing. That's the problem. I can't use you like that."

"OK, two hundred!"

He grabbed me by the shoulders and shook me severely. "You're on a mission man. This isn't what I came to get you for. Not really."

"Came to get me?"

"You don't understand," he moaned. Then his limp body snapped rigid and he broke into a run. "Just keep going, man. Follow the plan, stay on the golden itinerary. You'll get it."

"What plan?"

But he was already up the street, and Ezira was shrieking, "Strike a match, light a fuse, we only have the Earth to lose!"

Devastated by the cruel cutting off of intimacy, I stumbled back toward the hotel, suddenly feeling the rush of morphine as a wave of nausea. It was a sea change I'd experienced countless times before: the vast, warm tide of belonging that puts the flow of your blood in sync with the tides, suddenly dammed off in a new nauseous isolation, overflowing with a mean clamminess.

Back at the Mark Spencer, I stripped off my rain-drenched clothes and fell naked onto the bed. I'd slipped up to my neck into an abyss, which had become a funnel of sickly desire, and I'd been spiraling down it quite willingly, thrilled by the catalogue of characters. Now, suddenly, I was alone in the inky water, gasping for help, abandoned by everyone, the downward pull getting stronger and stronger. Floating in this state of malaise, I drifted into a momentary doze, until the ringing phone awoke me.

"You must let go of what happened, you must sleep peacefully," said the hypnotic voice. "Things are just beginning, and you'll need your strength."

"Who is this?"

"'Tis I." Suddenly I recognized the voice of Stapler.

"It's 3 o'clock in the morning!"

"Correct."[65]

"I'm confused," I whimpered, suddenly regressing into a vulnerable dependence. But why did I think I could appeal to him for help? "Tell me! What's happening?"

"You're getting used to a new environment," soothed Machu, with a pedagogic tone that could have been a parody. "Sleep now, so you can wake up fresh and shiny for what tomorrow promises."

"OK," I sniveled, astonished at the same time by my cowed manner.

---

65. Fortiphton's text was written on diary pages. If the correspondence between dates and entries are correct, he supposedly received this call on November 8, 2001, a date that, according to my agenda (all of which I save for a period of seven years for tax purposes) was the morning of a 7 AM parents' meeting at the nursery school that both Machu Stapler's son, Populus, and my youngest daughter, Evergreen, attend. Stapler arrived for the meeting on time, looking quite rested and well-groomed, which would cast strong doubt on the fact that he was making bizarre calls after three in the morning the night before.

VII

Dead(-Drunk) Reckoning

Long, but not so very long ago—before corporatized Seattle, startups and lattes, appropriationist art and health food emporiums, semiotics and power walking, gay marriage and websites, antioxidants, microwaves, four-wheel drives and colonoscopies—there was a quaint culture of mostly Finnish immigrants working to the bone at the wide mouth of the Columbia River, in the town of Astoria, who kept their bathtubs full of potatoes because they preferred the community sauna, didn't bother to learn much English, ruined their legs and backs in canneries or mills or lost a hand in sawmills and detested their employers; or so says the sagacious Narcissa W. Applegate, my learned research informant.[66] Under a cathedral of Douglas firs, if you'll excuse the overused metaphor, I now sped toward that destination, trying, with the aid of two more morphine tablets, to shake off the awful lure of Portland at night, which had threatened to engulf me like a moth in tar.

---

66. What a flagrant simplification of the material I took the trouble of sending him! I mailed him *reams* of information on the history of Finnish immigration to Astoria, Oregon, at the beginning of the twentieth century, including detailed material on the Finnish Socialist Federation Chapter. I suggest that anyone wanting serious reading on this topic consult the Immigration History Research Center at the University of Minnesota, which is rich in these documents, and not rely on Fortiphton as a source.

How can I explain the sickly obsession for Judas that had taken over my thoughts and emotions? For me he represented something turbulent and potentially cleansing, simmering beneath all the bland, a-historical qualities I'd accused the Pacific Northwest of having. I'd come to the realization that the majority of my complaints about cultural superficiality had to do with the self-invented quality of the place. Tucked away in the "upper-left-hand-corner" of the country, it had evaded the over-whelmingly historical, European influences of the East coast, including those bubbling melting pots of its old American cities, full of the racially opinionated and culturally saturated minds of the Old World, and produced instead a faltering, self-satisfied, self-invented culture from the dreams of its mostly Protestant, small-minded pioneers. It was an up-by-the-bootstraps operation that had now become America in the twenty-first century, a new ethos of self-determination that in some ways smacked of provincialism. With this polite and smiling monolith of practicality and social control, masked by alibis of self-reliance, inclusiveness and health-conscious temperance, the final flowering of the Protestant ethic and the spirit of capitalism, as set forth by Max Weber, was occurring. Or at least, that's what I'd thought.[67]

67. The author pitches wild volleys of references, turning me into the befuddled catcher. Max Weber, *The Protestant Ethic and the Spirit of Capitalism* (1905). Essentially a vicious attack on Protestant culture by an unhappy man. Weber perversely maintained that the Puritan emphasis on thrift was actually an incitement to capitalist acquisition. He argued that the Catholic Church was tolerant of lavish expenditure and display and didn't give a hoot about thriftiness, but that Protestant pride in "humble" work and saving led to high production and profits and the development of capitalism itself, sanctioned in their minds by God.

On the other hand, Judas, Ezira and their friends—perhaps even Walt Curtis—seemed to represent a hidden face of the land, something dark, irreverent and protesting, even potentially destructive of everything I claimed to hate. In my mind, at least, they were the embodiment of the hemlock and incense cedars, juniper, larches and firs covering the sides of the road like sinister fortresses. Their sheaths of green moss crept over everything, as if out of control, giving way at times to chilly cascades, primeval ferns or violently crashing waves. It was absurd, but at the sight of them, a kind of anti-community that I had a chance of becoming part of opened before me, like a maw or dark gulf.

Then why did I feel so left out? It was as if the region were just putting the finishing touches on its seamless, corporatized hegemony, complete with just enough of a gesture of sentimental respect for the nature around it; complete with fresh, new ways of curtailing libido; a rhetoric of impartiality that kept all the classes in their place; and imprinting sentimentality on the land they'd stolen from its aborigines. But at the same time, ragged marginals, fueled by deep resentment—hand in hand with savage Nature—could be plotting, perhaps even unconsciously, its violent downfall. How much I wanted to be a part of their imagined doomsday scenario!

Judas had returned the next day, somehow smuggling his unwashed odor past the hotel desk, to come knocking on the door of the room, the number of which I must have offered in my inebriated state. Begging for his monthly shower, he threw me the scraps of a striptease, before jumping into the hot spray with gasps of astonished relief. Afterward, he'd even consented to lie down towel-clad next to me on the bed, where he babbled about imagined future projects, which included a Nobel-prize-winning career in poetry, the rearing of several, eventually college-educated children and the establishment of a new American eco-political left.

Because of my current musings, it was the last item in that series that pricked up my ears, so I badgered him with questions about the current progress in his political ambitions, probing for some clue to the events of the last few days in my life, all of which I was becoming convinced were covertly connected. Were his aspirations, I wanted to know, somehow related to those years he'd spent in Eugene? Did he happen to know anyone named Walt Curtis or Machu Stapler?

Well, of course he knew Walt. Didn't everybody?

And hadn't he said he'd been waiting for me outside the hotel?

Who'd informed him of my presence?

He looked at me as if I were insane. Abruptly, he popped up from the bed, standing at an angle to flash his rear, in a last gesture of philanthropy, then shed his towel and pulled on his crusty jeans. Quite probably, my questions had caused him to panic.

He, on the other hand, thought the problem of nerves was all mine.

"Hey, a successful dude like you must have some killer Valium prescriptions, or something like that? Why don't you pop two or three."

In return for the generous medical advice, he requested another twenty, which he said he needed to do his laundry.

As he pocketed it—still bare-chested—I suddenly leapt forward and clung to him, while he wriggled in my arms. "Make me part of it," I begged.

Judas' body stiffened and he peeled me off with a shocked, distasteful frown.

"Huh?" was his answer.

With the alacrity of the urban nomad, he snaked into his tee shirt and sprinted to the door, gave me a leering wink, and then was down the hall. Despite myself, I ran to reopen the door and began calling desperately to him, "But I won't tell anybody, so why won't you trust me! Please, don't leave me out in the cold!" He kept going, of course, and my only alternative was to pack robotically, check out and reclaim the car.

I was headed for the next stop on my itinerary, Stapler's second house, in Astoria, located about a hundred miles west of Portland at the mouth of the Columbia River; and in my mind, which was suddenly saturated by my readings about the past, it wasn't the derelict shadow of its former glory as a major port and fishing town, nor any depressed city hoping to resuscitate itself through the tourist trade.[68] None of this mattered at all, because by now I was firmly ensconced in my imagination, and all I could think of was the bawdy, brawling Astoria of the past, filled with hard-drinking sailors and sawmill workers; cruel, exploitive shipping magnates living in drafty Victorian mansions on the hill; a brothel for sailors near the harbor; and fierce Scandinavian laborers, who

---

68. I suppose this understatement serves the author's wild narrative purposes; but truth is, Astoria, where I keep a country house, has shown vital signs of real recovery lately. It's true that the former salmon-fishing and trading center has seen some hard times, but its low rents and wonderful real estate bargains are attracting a whole new generation of poets, pottery-makers and restaurateurs, proof again that we Northwesterners know how to reinvent ourselves.

were secretly assembling bricks and bats to give the cannery and mill bosses a run for their money. It had to be so: if I could discover no link between the punkish disenfranchised of today and the surly activists of yore, life wouldn't be worth living.

Here, I thought, as I drove into town past lapping gray waves, which hemmed in the narrow downtown area next to the steep residential streets to the south, I would somehow bring history alive again.

I turned up one of those steep inclines toward Stapler's ramshackle Victorian mansion, suddenly feeling quite happy to be in the oldest U.S. settlement in the entire West. The house, once gracious and stately, was in dire need of repair; it had become a dowdy old spinster, full of cobwebs and busted-spring furniture. Although it was unlocked, as if expecting visitors, it wasn't particularly welcoming with its thermostat set to 62. The first thing I did was twirl the dial up to 76. I could hear the old furnace groan as if in astonished protest, then burst into rumbling flames I knew would soon make the place toasty. Stapler had said he had no intention of coming out until the following weekend and had crisply requested I be sparing with the heat. But no one would know until the bill came. By then I'd be back in New York, I figured; let them take it out of my royalties.

The next thing I headed for was the liquor cabinet. It was quite well stocked, to my delight. I poured myself a scotch and took a sip to swallow a morphine tablet, then headed for the sinking porch, which creaked under my feet. Since the house hadn't warmed up yet, I'd be no less comfortable in the damp and drizzle. It was noon, and the view in the encroaching fog revealed only the sharp edges of roofs, between which one could catch glimpses of the leaden water of the mouth of the river. However, in some areas of the sky, the droplet-saturated air caught the rays of a struggling sun and diffused them into a lustrous wash. This was reflected in the wet, black asphalt to create a disorienting, mirror-like sensation, similar to the one achieved by staring directly into silver. Dimensions and directions get lost in the watery glare, and you plunge into its metallic dispersal. With the help of the scotch and the morphine, I floated into this melancholy evanescence, until a female voice startled me out of the liquid feeling.

Claiming to have been sent by Stapler as a sort of local guide was an ancient, shriveled woman with elfin eyes and crudely cropped hair, who introduced herself as Delilah. Was I ready for a trip into the heart of Astoria? she wanted to know. But first, she said, eyeing the scotch, would I be willing to supply a little "fuel"?

I felt surprisingly profligate with the borrowed bottle, and I led the old witch inside to pour her a stiff one. As we entered, her wrinkled face burst into an expression of astonishment. Was I planning on opening a sauna? For her, the place was stifling! I compromised by turning the thermostat down to 69, and we settled into one of the broken-down couches in the high-ceilinged Victorian parlor. She clutched the glass of scotch with knobby, arthritic hands and toasted me with the Finnish expression, "Kippis!" Then she bottomed up faster than I could raise my glass to my lips.

A half hour later, we were in Delilah's strangely well-preserved Studebaker, heading up Coxcomb Hill toward the Astoria Column. Frail as she looked, she pushed the clutch into second like a truck driver, muttering a few expletives when it stalled for a moment and coughed halfway up.

Half totem pole and half W.P.A. mural, the stately column, which looked expertly carved in intaglio, was a monument to

Caucasian land-grabbing schemes throughout the continent. Delilah's surprisingly frigid fingers grabbed my forearm, leading me to the steps inside it, which spiraled to a dizzying height of 125 feet, promising a breathtaking view of Youngs Bay. I heard her gasp and wheeze as we struggled up those stairs, but each time I took her arm, she shook it off with hostility.

When we reached the top, both of us were winded; the sun had suddenly broken through the clouds, revealing one of the oldest faces I'd ever seen. Above a mass of deep wrinkles were two cataract-clouded blue eyes; and from them glimmered a silvery light, producing the same effect as the silver-tinged sky of Astoria I'd noticed earlier. Perhaps I imagined that the eyes seemed to be sizing me up; and her mouth, which was little more than a thin, rigid line, seemed to curl at the corners with a hint of perverse amusement.

"How... old are you, Delilah?" I heard myself blurting indecorously.

"A hundred and two," she barked. "Now put that behind your ears and cogitate on it!"

Back in the Studebaker, we headed for what Delilah termed "the only darned establishment still worth seeing in this town," the Labor Temple and Café, a bar that I assumed had once held festivities for exhausted salmon canners, shipyard workers, sailors and mill workers in Astoria's heyday as an industrial beehive. Its upper walls were lined with the severed heads of some big-antlered moose and a single spotted bobcat. One wall held hundreds of photos of the labor past during the 20s, 30s, 40s and 50s: hale and hearty Scandinavians dressed in their Sunday best crowded around tables holding pitchers of beer, their open, strangely placid faces turned obligingly toward the camera, with just a hint of exhaustion in their liquid eyes. All this was a part of Delilah's roots, I'd soon find out; for she launched into a tale that endeared her to me almost immediately, turning her from a cranky crone into something frail and waifish.

Delilah was part of the large community of people of Finnish extraction who still lived in Astoria, many of whom had ancestors who'd been squashed by the government and the industrialists during the climax of the labor movement. She was, in fact, no real Delilah, but a Finnish immigrant, appropriately named Aamu, who'd come to work in a salmon cannery at the age of thirteen and had moonlighted more than eighty years ago in the offices of the Finnish Communist newspaper *Toveritar*,[69] a publication with strong connections to the Wobblies, as well as other labor organizations.

During the year she worked there—from 1918 to 1919—the Wobblies sometimes used the offices of *Toveritar* to meet and plan strategy. It was around the time of the Centralia Massacre[70]—either before or after, Delilah, or Aamu, wasn't

---

69. Finnish for "Woman Comrade." It was the sister newspaper of "Toveri," or "Comrade."

70. On November 11, 1919, in Centralia, Washington, an ultra-left Industrial Workers of the World (I.W.W.) hall was raided by a small group of Legionnaires who'd broken away from a parade. Expecting the raid, the members of the I.W.W., or Wobblies, as they were known, were armed and ready. No one knows who fired first, but two Legionnaires were killed. One of the Wobblies, Wesley Everest, was later apprehended at the Skookumchuck River, and was, unfortunately, castrated and hung. In Centralia today, there's a stirring monument to the fallen Legionnaires that is certainly worth seeing if you happen to be in the area.

sure—that local officials arrived to arrest all of the paper's editors. Aamu, who was only sixteen, hid under a desk to avoid the authorities, and when her editor friends who'd been rounded up were deported back to Finland, she became demoralized and frightened.

Feeling the same kind of pressure, another group of labor activists, who were her acquaintances, and who felt that the company stores were fleecing cannery and mill workers of their meager salaries (they called these company stores "robber-saries"), decided to leave the country willingly and migrate to Russia to become a part of the new revolution. Aamu quickly packed a trunk, resolved to go with them; but the day the boat left, she was suddenly seized with uncertainty. She spent the afternoon trembling in the community sauna, in all her clothes, her packed bags next to her. She figured correctly that it would be the last place her departing friends would look, and she was right, for the majority had gathered in front of her house, calling up toward the attic their pleas for her to come with them.

"Aamu, tulla!"

Several years later, she realized she'd made the right decision; most of the idealistic Communist workers who left on that trip were eventually deported by Stalin to a gulag.

Reckoning that the labor movement had been all but crushed in Astoria, Aamu developed a strong dislike for the place, which was fraught with too many terrifying memories of betrayal. She moved to Coal Creek, in Cowlitz County, several miles inland from the Columbia River, in Washington State, and got work on a potato farm. In Coal Creek, a small Finnish community that hadn't yet lost its socialist ideals held sway.

There were weekend parties at the dance hall and a weekly afternoon sauna, in which Aamu's best girlfriend, Kate Niemis, would swat her with red cedar switches to improve her already excellent circulation.

It wasn't long before Paavo Moilanen, a local whose only job was to go from home to home delivering gossip, took an interest in her rosy cheeks. But radical Aamu was more interested in a virtual newcomer, a non-Finn named Bill Lassoter, who was blind and had run a newsstand in Centralia that sold papers espousing the views of the Wobblies and other subversive tracts. He'd been rounded up twice by town vigilantes and driven without his possessions to another county; each time he'd found his way back and continued to sell the papers. However, two months in jail on trumped-up charges and the subsequent Centralia Massacre had sent a clear message that there was no more future for him in Centralia than a tar and feathering. With the aid of his dog, he'd made it across forest trails to Coal Creek, where he arrived with a broken leg, multiple briar lacerations and a starving dog, and was welcomed by the Finnish radicals.

Poor Aamu had made every choice in her young life as the result of compassionate impulses: the gnarled, prematurely aged body of thirty-four-year-old Tom Lassiter and the two cloudy orbs of his blind eyes led to another. Nonetheless, hard-drinking, hard-working and communal as the Finns were, they were not a group who easily tolerated illegitimate pregnancies. After learning she was with child, blind Bill disappeared again into the woods. There was nothing for Aamu to do but come back to Astoria and hope that people would believe her story of widowhood and a mourned husband.

Luckily, a Finnish sailor who was a new immigrant did believe it, and he and Aamu were married five months before the child was born. This was the start of three more generations who'd stayed in the area. All of them had grown up in poverty in a family that sought its livelihood primarily from the sea and that included alcoholic fathers who were boatswains or flour mill workers, during a time when both industries were in sharp decline.

Aamu herself currently lived in a converted barn. But now her own eighty-eight-year-old daughter was dying of lung cancer, and because Aamu and her great-grandson were the only relatives left in the area, they'd probably soon move in together into Aamu's daughter's small, weather-beaten row house.

By the time this tale was finished, we were heading in Aamu's pickup for the docks because, as she explained, she had a very special surprise in store for me, something she'd come up with on the promptings of Stapler. We were going on a boat ride. Her great-grandson, Jukku, whom most people called Johnny, had just received his certificate as a bar pilot and would be guiding his first Japanese container ship under the Astoria Bridge.[71]

It was a lucrative, but potentially very dangerous, job. Hidden under the swirling waters of the river's enormous mouth were treacherous bars, which could act like sucking mouths that created huge, voracious swells. A good number of even experienced sailors had met their death there, riding one moment on the flat surface of the sea, which seemed as stable as a floor, and

---

71. The 4.1 mile bridge on US 101 that joins Oregon to Washington State, across the mouth of the Columbia, and is the longest continuous truss bridge in the world! Why doesn't Fortiphton provide such essential information in a travel narrative?

then suddenly swooning downward, with enormous walls of liquid rising up menacingly on either side. That's why a supply of highly trained local captains were needed in Astoria, to get the ships safely past the river mouth and take it upstream.

The thought of our upcoming adventure sent a thrill coursing down my spine, and I wondered, perhaps wildly, how such an experience could have been prepared for me without Stapler having known the spiritual trajectory I had been traveling. Was not the river, with its predictable downstream course, lined on either side by the punctilious settlements of commerce, the perfect objective correlative of the bland cultural tyranny I so deplored? And wasn't it just and natural that when it met the swirling id of the sea, a violent and ungovernable reaction should occur? But how, in a million years, could all of those who seemed to be shaping my trip out here realize that this represented the distillation of my imaginings, that I myself had been slipping downstream on a dull, predictable path of aging, only to find myself suddenly facing an inexplicable dark unmooring, full of exciting, perhaps treacherous currents?

Aamu had parked the car a few blocks from the pilots' pier, to give me a better feeling of downtown, I assumed; and as we walked past the Maritime Museum on a neighboring wharf, I saw that the adjoining harbor, which was full of sailboats and recreational cruisers, had been invaded by a colony of enormous sea walruses. They were sprawled on the docks as if drugged, some belly up, morosely staring at the heavens. At the sound of our walking by, several of these tubby mammoths flipped to a standing position with surprising speed and charged along the dock toward us with raucous, rageful honks. Inebriated as we were, both Aamu and I broke into startled laughter, and together, our noise and the animals' seemed to shatter the moist air as if it were made of glass.

With this feeling of libido and spontaneity rippling through me, I followed Aamu onto the small pilot boat, which immediately took off from the dock and headed toward the bridge. Three men were with us, the driver of the pilot boat, his assistant, and the river pilot. According to the usual procedure, Aamu's great-grandson Johnny, the bar pilot, had been driven out earlier beyond the bars to meet a container ship coming from Japan. He would navigate the freighter past the bars and under the bridge, whereupon we would meet him at the ship with the river pilot. It was the river pilot's job to relieve Johnny and then guide the ship a hundred miles along the river to Portland. Both bar pilot and river pilot had months of rigorous training under their belts. Only they, and not, for example, the Japanese captain of the freighter, knew every current, inlet and shallow of the Columbia and its mouth, a necessity for getting it safely from the ocean to Portland.

The light, euphoric feeling of release still dominated my body as we skipped across the waves toward a speck in the distance. Droplets of rain made glimmering, blurred patterns against the windshield of the boat. Its pilot was in a merry mood, as well, spouting river tales of past gales and sailor bloopers, flirting with Aamu, whom he'd known since he was a child, as if she were an attractive young filly, by peppering her with harmless, macho banter. Each time he turned to gaze out the water-spattered windshield, Aamu would make comic gestures of contempt in his direction, then swiftly slip a flask that she'd filled with my editor's scotch from her purse, take a quick swig and pass it to me.

Slowly, the ship we were heading for came into view, enlarging almost imperceptibly, until it finally revealed its full 900-foot length, the size of three city blocks. It was a faceless, windowless gray hulk, rising several stories above the level of the sea—like a monstrous steel anvil that had the miraculous ability to float on the surface of water. The closer we came, the more its menace increased, dwarfing our small pilot's craft to the proportions of a fly, making it clear that if just the wrong swell of water were to thrust us against it, it would shatter us like a sledge hammer could crystal. There it stood, almost motionless, as if glued to the ocean, a fragile rope ladder hanging from its wall of a side like a spider web.

"They must be carrying, say, about 4,000 Toyotas," said the driver of our boat with a slightly ironic gloat. "Looks pretty stable now, but when they get out to sea, they're so top heavy that they really roll."

The gray, floating mammoth sent a shiver of awe through me, not so much from the imminent danger of getting close to such massive bulk, but from the realization that every feature, aside from its utilitarian function, was designed to repulse. Faceless and sealed to the environment, its only purpose was to protect and transfer 6,000 tons of steel, plastic and glass; and inside this windowless prison, which moved at only 22 miles per hour at top speed, was a crew of about 12 or 15, who spent several probably dismal months at sea. It was commerce at its ugliest and most oppressive; but this didn't mean that it, as well, couldn't be deceived and destroyed by the vortex at which nature met civilization. The thought of this afforded me a perverse pleasure.

Our small craft inched toward the hulk more and more

slowly until we were side by side, almost touching. Then the river pilot bid us a cheery goodbye and hopped onto our deck. Seizing the rope ladder hanging from the container ship, he climbed up the side of the mammoth ship with the agility of a monkey.

According to the driver of our boat, we now had to wait several minutes during which the bar pilot, finished with his task, presented the river pilot to the Japanese captain, and turned over direction of the freighter up the Columbia River to him. Then the bar pilot, who was Delilah's great-grandson Johnny, would come back down the ladder and we'd transport him back to shore.

Just as predicted, a body appeared at the top of the container ship's rope ladder. It moved even faster than the one that had gone up, because it was younger and slimmer. As it stepped from the bottom of the ladder onto our deck, I caught a glimpse of the oval face beneath the black wool cap. It was beaming with excitement, probably from the fact of having successfully accomplished its first journey past the bars.

It was a stirringly handsome face, strong and sculpted, with just a touch of Billy Budd vulnerability; or at least that's how I saw it in the trembling excitement of the moment. Then the shadow of a darker thrill passed through me as I studied the large, blue, tempestuous eyes, which seemed to hold that same wild energy I'd seen earlier on this trip and been so startled and confused by. My entire soul fell into those eyes, and my whole journey compressed in my mind into one wordless, insane realization that I cannot describe.[72]

---

72. What can I say!

There was, however, another surprise in store for me. Instead of pulling away, our boat hovered, still unmoving, inches away from the container ship.

"Aren't we going now?" I ventured.

The question was met with a tense silence.

By now Johnny, the bar pilot, had entered the boat. Was I imagining that he kept staring at me with a playful, teasing smile? Aamu spit out some cursory introductions, after which silence reigned again, while our boat stayed inexplicably in place and Johnny kept staring at me, almost challengingly, I thought. To avoid his glance, I studied his large, dry, but some-how sensitive-looking hands, letting my eye trail from them up his arms to the curves of his muscular shoulders. Then my gaze slid downwards along his broad, flat chest, pausing irresistibly at his crotch to discover that the material of his pants was raised over a flattened bulge, possibly an erection.

Just a few moments later, another figure appeared at the top of the rope ladder and scrambled down to our deck even faster than Johnny had. He was dressed like the two pilots, in down jacket and work boots; but he had tied a black bandana around his chin, which had been pulled up to the level of the top of his nose. As he hopped onto our deck, a second, almost identically dressed figure appeared at the top of the rope ladder; and it, too, scrambled down to our boat. Both of them were much smaller than Johnny, wiry and crouched, as if ready to leap up and bolt at any moment.

Immediately Aamu extracted her flask, and both strangers in bandanas took a gulp from it. Tension was as thick as a knife as we headed back to Astoria. No one had introduced me to the two extra passengers. The waves had risen, and we leapt swiftly over them, like a weighted cork; but while the other passengers and I were tossed upward a bit each time we hit a wave, the two strangers remained in place, their knees spread, their feet planted firmly on the floor. They had still not removed their bandanas; and everyone in the boat seemed to avoid their and my glance, except for Aamu and her great-grandson, who seemed to be gazing at me with a gloating, almost jubilant expectation.

As soon as we got back to shore, the two extra passengers scrambled to the deck and hopped onto the dock, sprinting toward the street until they disappeared. It was as if they hadn't existed. The thickness of tension suddenly broke, and the driver of our boat resumed his corny, homey banter. Aamu began chattering in her croaky voice about celebrating her great-grandson's first successful run by taking him back to the Labor Temple and Café for a few more drinks. She commanded me to meet them there in an hour. "You just got to," she bid me severely.

"Delilah," I managed to croak out, "who were those other two men?"

She let out a raucous peal of laughter, as if my question were absurd, and Johnny turned away to gaze at the street. "You know," she said offhandedly, avoiding my eyes, "sailors used to have a ball when they finally got to port. It made up for all those dreary days at sea. Nowadays, with the terrorist threat and all, most of 'em are confined to the ship."

"But who were they?"

A note of exasperation crept into her voice. "Silly man from another land, there's still a lot of solidarity among people of the sea." And with that, she waved goodbye, but not until her great-grandson, to my astonishment, had given me a playful slap on the ass.[73]

It was growing dark as I trudged back up the hill to Stapler's house. Now the setting sun had become powerful enough to inject strong shafts of rose through the watery sky, which seemed to writhe with the pleasure of it. Then the play of light deepened into a lid that weighed heavily on the city, congealing into a black viscosity that made it hard to see my feet below me.

The house, which I'd left set at 72 degrees, was toasty as I liked it. As was my wont when I was indoors, I kicked off my shoes and stripped down to my underwear. My memory of what had just happened seemed to crawl over me like insects, or was it like the feeling of colliding with a spider web in the dark: invisible sticky strands that are impossible to remove and cling in places that are difficult to pinpoint? For the first time, a terrible sense of confinement began to close in, the feeling of becoming a pawn in someone else's diabolic game; and the fact

---

73. I'll admit that, given today's political climate, I was, naturally, rather distressed to read these allegations. That's why—despite my strong doubts about the reliability of the source—I immediately brought the information to the local authorities in Astoria and forwarded a copy to the attorney general. The reaction in both quarters was one of disbelieving hilarity, bordering on contempt. As if talking to a child, they explained the various security systems in line to prevent non-American merchant marines from leaving a ship without permission. I left headquarters in Astoria feeling like a laughing stock, because it was clear that they took my information as the ravings of a hysterical woman. I should have known better than to give any credence to Fortiphton's increasingly preposterous claims—much less identify myself with any of them publicly.

that I seemed to be the last to know suddenly filled me with an impotent rage.

In the throes of a cold panic, afraid that even my old friend Walt was part of all this, I ended up calling for the first and last time that Applegate woman, my research source, because I couldn't think of anybody else to whom to appeal.

It turned out to be a healthy reality check. In an arch and frigid voice of cordiality, she responded to my increasingly wild claims with bland "oh's," and "really's?"[74] Her detachment, the shrewish sense of judgment hiding beneath her polite exclamations, especially when I mentioned the imbibing of too much alcohol (I wouldn't have dared mention the morphine) and the obvious lack of compassion or true caring beneath her veneer of a concerned and helpful good citizen, reaffirmed my cynicism about the ruling classes of this region; and with a renewed sense of the sardonic, a little equilibrium returned. If a woman who billed herself as a Western cultural activist and the sacred

---

74. I barely feel the need to point out what a deranged fabrication this is. The truth is that I was *very* concerned with the slurred, obviously disturbed voice that called me into the house in the middle of my seven-year-old daughter Liberty's soccer practice—so concerned that I immediately phoned his editor and said that he must be removed immediately from the assignment and sent back East, with a firm urging to seek psychiatric help. I'll admit, that to make my case, I finally revealed to Machu what I knew about Fortiphton's recent criminal past. But even after supplying that information, to my great surprise, Machu expressed the opinion that such imaginings were harmless and would perhaps even add an element of creative imagination to the book! He insisted that nothing should be done at the current time. How I wish he'd taken my warnings more seriously!

guardian of its hallowed history[75] didn't seem to care about alien infiltrators or primitivist eco-terrorists, why should I? But I certainly didn't plan to show up at the Labor Temple and Café; they could find another East Coast imbecile to use as their patsy.

I stalked back and forth in my underwear in the dark house, wind-milling my arms at invisible fears, then hurried to my luggage to extract another tablet of morphine. I threw open the door of the walnut cabinet bar, which struck the wall, chipping the plaster. Grabbing what was left of the scotch, I swilled it down, then doubled over coughing, letting the bottle crash to the floor.

It was in this tortured position that I noticed the seashell on the floor below the couch, and something metallic gleaming from it. The shell held a large key, the classic type that had been used over eighty years ago. That's when I realized I hadn't yet bothered to examine the house.

Muttering and with head bowed, I walked up the stairs in the dark until my forehead collided painfully against a door. At first the key didn't seem to fit; but after jiggling the handle and key at the same time, I felt the door give and pushed it open. Behind it, and leading to the attic, was a narrow, very steep flight of more stairs, almost vertical, of a type I'd seen only in the cramped houses lining the canals of Amsterdam. In my inebriated state of bewilderment and rage, it was all I could do to pull myself up them, sputtering for breath.

At the top, I fumbled for a light switch and flipped it on, which illuminated only half of the immense space. Beneath the sloping walls of the attic was a single gigantic room, which

---

75. Pure fabrication. I've never made such extravagant claims!

looked almost like an army barracks, mostly because of the rows of about thirty cots that filled the center. The walls were lined with books. Stooping under the sloping sides of the roof to examine them, I began scanning the titles. Everything was impeccably arranged, in alphabetical order: from Bakunin, Bey and Goldman to Debord and Zerzan; but pop marginals were there, as well, such as McVeigh and Manson. Stacks of clippings recounting attacks and arrests that went all the way back to the Symbionese Liberation Army and the Panthers had been carefully paper-clipped together in folders.

At the farther end of the room, which was still plunged into gloom, was a large, white board on a wooden easel, blocking the triangular window, the kind of board used in kindergartens on which you could write with a felt-tip pen and then erase by wiping. On it, in the semi-darkness, was a childishly executed color drawing.

I stumbled toward the light switch on the opposite wall and flipped it on. A brass Revere chandelier, hanging precariously from the ceiling and outfitted with flame-shaped bulbs, illuminated the room with a wan glow.

On the white board was a felt-tip map of the Oregon coast. It was obvious that it had been painstakingly but rather inaccurately copied and enlarged from a smaller map in a book, in an artless attempt to reproduce the many inlets and tiny peninsulas that jutted from the shore. Red dots had been used to indicate the cities, and blue lines depicted the highways connecting them.

It took me a moment to realize that the green line running north/south was a visual rendering of my itinerary. There it was, beginning at a little asterisk next to the city of Seattle, advancing down along the Washington and Oregon coasts to Portland, then dropping further down to Eugene and back up to Portland, zigzagging west to Astoria and then across the bridge to Washington State on toward Canada.

Through the numbness of alcohol and morphine, I stared dazedly at it, mouthing the strange phrases and terms in parentheses next to the stops:

1) Pre-Assignment: New York—Background Investigation

2) Seattle: Brush Contact With Target—Cold Approach

3) Portland: Maintain Cover—Plant Drugs If Necessary

4) Eugene: First Contact with Cell—Begin Biographic Leverage

5) Portland: Honey Trap (Use Raven[76] for Co-option)

6) Astoria: Employ Usual Stringer; Contact Is To Maintain Deep Cover; Some Disinformation Could Prove Helpful; Raven May Use Pressure

7) Aberdeen: Continue Attempt at Re-Education

8) Port Angeles: Target Should Be Ready for Enlistment (Employ Multiple Ravens Again, If Necessary); If Recruitment Negative, Burn[77]

9) La Push: End of Assignment

---

76. Male prostitute working in collusion with an espionage agent.

77. Slang term for deliberate sacrificing of an intelligence agent, usually a newbie.

VIII

The Troll Under the Bridge

Of course, there was no bunker-like attic or clandestine itinerary, and probably no second or third bandana-clad figure coming down from the rope ladder after the bar pilot. Why should anyone believe me? Why should I believe myself when I know my blood was saturated with more alcohol and morphine than even I was used to imbibing, when I found myself lying in my underwear among shards of glass from the broken scotch bottle in the middle of the downstairs living room floor the next morning, without any memory of getting back down there, if I had, indeed, ever gone up.[78]

Despite my penchant for self-destruction, a sense of prideful contempt for the area persisted beneath my disintegration; I wasn't about to let the Western provinces get the better of this shrewd Eastcoaster. My hosts didn't know it yet, but my "tour" was over. I'd drive the heap of junk they'd assigned to me—probably as a demoralizing tactic—straight to the Portland airport, abandon it there and use the rest of my slim budget for a one-way ticket back to New York.

Moments later, however, as I was loading the rest of Stapler's liquor supply into my duffle bag, I felt a large, rough hand with a strangely sensitive touch gently caressing the back of my neck with its callused fingers. Then the hand grasped my neck and turned me around, after which I saw enormous wild blue eyes staring into mine. They were, I decided, the eyes of Delilah/

---

78. Yes, admit it!

Aamu's great-grandson, Jukka, if you'll allow me to use his Finnish name, and they pulled me toward him with a strange magnetism, until my lips were crushed against his, tasting the flavor of the licorice Snus he kept in his mouth between cheek and gums, then opening to the plunge of his tongue.

After we pulled away, the look on his face was in no way in accordance with the amorous gesture he'd just completed. His features were hardened into a blank, militaristic impassivity, and the blue eyes had dulled into the impenetrable color of tin. "I've received instructions," he said, "from your editor. He doesn't believe his car can make it all the way to Vancouver, so you'll be leaving it here and riding with me in my jeep for the rest of the itinerary."

Without answering, I took a step to the side so that I was in line with the open door behind him, through which the first truly sunny day of my visit glared; but he rapidly shifted his position, forming a barrier between me and that portal of freedom.

"Get your bag," he required in a flat, staccato voice that bordered on the sullen, then folded his arms over a puffy chest and stood blocking the door with legs astride. I'll never forget the image of his backlit, unmoving, booted body, in its khaki green clothing, transformed into a two-dimensional dark silhouette by the constriction of my pupils to the harsh light outside the door. It changed everything around it into a fable, within which he became the central golem. "You should have showed up at the Labor Temple and Café last night," was all he said. "We were expecting you." The severity of his tone was enough to make me follow wordlessly with my bag to the jeep.

It rattled down the steep incline toward the water and then swerved left toward the bridge. Jukka had lapsed into a stony silence, which complemented my emerging sense of being held prisoner. He answered my few questions in monosyllables or short sentences, almost the way a petty officer briefs an underling. In such a situation, others might be fixated on the possibilities for escaping or, at least, be trying to unravel the web of manipulation that had put them in this perplexing position. But amazingly, my entire mind was occupied by the notions with which I'd arrived in this region and how artlessly "off" every impression was that I'd had.

This was all I thought about as we drove over the Astoria Bridge toward Washington State, not so very far above the steel-gray, thrashing waves of the mouth of the Columbia below. It was a thrilling experience, almost like driving across the surface of the water itself, because of the relative thinness and astonishing length of this truss bridge.

We were headed, Jukka informed me, for the eastern end of Grays Harbor, on the banks of the Chehalis and Wishkah Rivers, to pick up a "shipment" (human, I suspected) before continuing on to Port Angeles; and as the spray stung my face through the open windows of the jeep, I had the impression that I was finally understanding this region for the very first time. It was neither an Edenic natural paradise nor a smug, opportunist hub of commerce, but actually an accidental, brilliantly grotesque collision between the two. Again and again in the fine mist of sea and rain, huge stretches of forest or water would hypnotize me into a state of awed surrender, whether I saw the gloomy, totalitarian majesty of a stand of old Douglas firs or waves slashing a desolate, pebbly shore. Then all this would be interrupted suddenly by the baldness of a clear-cut hill or the sinister, smoke-spewing stacks of the juggernaut of a power plant. Unlike the East, where, in many places, such sights had long ago tamed and supplanted nature, here the struggle aggressively raged in all its blatant and elemental vulgarity.

Everything seemed accidental and random, and at moments I chastised myself for my naiveté in thinking that I'd been assigned to an insipid territory that was energetically working in an orderly manner to spread the commoditized North American dream. No, by some accident I'd fallen upon another form of chaos—I, the critic who had always lauded the chaotic adventure of the Eastern urban scene. My thoughts scanned the pages of reading I'd accomplished about the region's history, suddenly realizing that everything here was the product of the miracle of chance, that the reason the people seemed like ciphers was because the tumultuous question of civilization's outcome raged within them all.

This was a place—I finally had to admit—of violence and struggle, a thrillingly ugly battle between the land and humans that produced a rich, stupefying sensory experience. Here there would never be a chance for genuine order; only the snarl of nature echoed by the discontent of the human condition—and all of it hiding under a featureless mask of progressivism because the people here were well aware that their struggle could never be completely expressed in words.[79]

---

79. God help this errant soul. Was it some exaggerated duty I felt as a researcher to go through the motions of verifying these claims? I suppressed the urge to chuck the whole manuscript in the garbage and called poor, busy Machu Stapler one more time. Is it really necessary to emphasize the fact that his record of service to our community makes me trust him implicitly? Of course, he confirmed all my suspicions by assuring me that he knows of no centenarian with a great-grandson of a bar pilot in Astoria and had merely asked a young neighbor, on leave from the Armed Forces, to loan Fortiphton his jeep for the rest of the trip—so that Machu could reclaim the car he needed when he came to Astoria the following weekend. Even if these ravings were nothing more than the stuff of good fiction, I wouldn't complain; but it's become too painfully clear that they lack any literary value whatsoever.

Having read a fair amount of literature about the next stop on my itinerary, I knew what to expect of Aberdeen, the small city at the eastern end of Grays Harbor: a drab southern Washington mill town not many miles from the other side of the Astoria bridge, population approximately 17,000, a good number of whom, after losing their jobs in the lumber industry, must have sunk into alcoholism, which the surprising number of taverns and bars in the nearly deserted downtown area clearly confirmed.

Once upon a time near the beginning of the twentieth century, Aberdeen and its twin city of Hoquiam had been lusty boomtowns, when their substantial immigrant population, abundant salmon, plentiful forests and position on the Chehalis River kept their canneries, shipyards and mills humming. But the bust of the 1930s was a blow from which Aberdeen had never recovered, and its decline had been mostly steady since that time.

Jukka parked the jeep on the main street, informing me that we were about to "make our choices from the shipment." He led me into the only establishment in downtown Aberdeen that seemed to have any activity: a pool-hall-cum-newsstand in which a collection of savage male adolescents, fated for dereliction and homelessness, loitered, playing pool, bumming cigarettes and breaking into occasional scuffles until the proprietor, a pallid, middle-aged, blonde woman with ringed eyes, bellowed at them over the sound of The Doors' *People Are Strange*.

Never before, even in the ghettoes of the East, had I seen such ebullient desperation. Scraggly-haired and scrawny, jittery with rageful anxiety, the shoulders of their shirts and their cigarettes drenched by the rain outside, they marched up and down the length of the pool table, often hitting the ball with such force that it went flying off to strike a wall, an event that produced catcalls of perverse jubilation. Others stared glumly with slackened mouths at the "game" in process, calling out acidic insults every time someone missed a shot.

The majority had the habit of rubbing their crotches during an idle moment, not in any gesture of sexuality but in the bored spirit of passing time evoked by a cat licking its fur. They were speed freaks, I assumed; but they were also tied to the whipping posts of a failing industry. They had more than likely been abused at home by working class parents who were victims of the new service economy, who wore sweatshirts calling for the frying of the spotted owl and spent the endless unemployed rainy season paging through copies of *Soldier of Fortune* magazine, which one of the youths sat perusing at that very moment.

Jukka picked several of them, drew them into a corner of the pool hall and whispered an inaudible proposition into their ears. I sat across the room studying them, interrupted regularly by one or another bumming a cigarette, until my pack was depleted, while I continued my meditation on my journey in a new demoralized way. Looking at it as a whole, it represented a descent—from the brittle, satirical sense of superiority I'd arrived with, to a progressive state of humiliation and bewilderment. Relentlessly, albeit deliriously, I'd moved down the social scale closer and closer to the region's vagrants, who were all that interested me, but whose international culture of poverty told no more about the region than the same group of disenfranchised marginals in any area of the world.

Once again, I was seized by the impulse to escape the subversive activities of this outfit, which now seemed to have become increasingly apparent at each stage in the journey. No, there'd be no book or entrapment. I was through with my "research." There had to be a moment when Jukka would forget his vigilance.

Jukka's new recruits, he informed me, would meet us the following morning at the motel he'd chosen for us. It was yet another of the colorless establishments with which we're all familiar, one of many on a garish boulevard that competed with each other with neon signs promising pleasures that ranged from waterbeds and mini-gyms to cable TV. The one we turned into was less than a block from the local casino, and Jukka specified that it be booked in my name, since he was, undoubtedly, traveling under cover.

It was very early evening when we checked in, even too soon for dinner. Despite the orangey light of the bedside lamp, Jukka's perky features—which included a small, regular nose; dimpled chin; blue, enormously lidded eyes; and pink, sinuous lips—suddenly took on an exhausted pallor. Then a strange gleam of compassion crept into his formerly opaque irises, and he gently motioned me to him on the bed.

Quite rapidly, his entire face was contaminated by this delicate new emotion; he took my head in both enormous callused hands and stared into my face with a disturbing frankness. The words that followed astounded me, because despite their liberal use of euphemisms, they contained an uncanny awareness of my own mental processes. I seemed to be, he said, about to fail at the accomplishment of the project for which I'd been drafted.[80] This,

---

80. Which was to write a travelogue. That's all, I can assure you.

he had to admit, was causing him an uncustomary feeling of consternation. It was not often the case that he developed a sense of protectiveness about his "targets." It was, in fact, downright unprofessional of him. Nevertheless, the task he'd have to perform if I did not swiftly progress in my "re-education" was one that he now dreaded.

Taking a different tack, he made some references to the prejudices with which I had arrived but said he wanted to make it clear that he was, in fact, quite impressed by my intelligence. However, I seemed to have a tendency for a certain kind of emotionality that the "drafters" hadn't considered. I wouldn't call the tone that followed "pleading," but the tiny tremor in his voice rather closely resembled it. All I had to do, he explained, was open myself to the struggle of the people of this region. Then his voice darkened, returning to its robotic frigidity, as he added, with a strange casualness, "Otherwise you're finished."

I suppose that the gesture that came next was an attempt to color what he'd said as convincing. I won't describe it in detail because none of this really has much relevance to my story. I won't dwell on every feature of his deliriously silken, wiry body, nor the two hard melons of his buttocks, which tightened into steel with each thrust into me as we lay together on the still-made bed, because I doubt anyone would believe me, and because my state of confusion at the time would not make me a very reliable narrator. I will admit, however, that despite the swooning surrender necessary to accommodate such maneuvers, I did not lapse completely into the manipulated subject that was the intended goal, because shortly after he fell asleep, I crept to retrieve his olive khakis on the floor and gently extracted the key to the jeep. Then, with no idea of where it would take me, I sped up East Market Street and northwest on East 2nd, where I found myself in a lower class residential neighborhood and a frustrating cul-de-sac.

I threw the jeep into Park and sat anxiously staring through the dirty windshield at the eternal drizzle, wondering about the easiest way to find egress. Those thoughts were quickly interrupted by the sight in my rearview mirror of an approaching taxi, quite far off, but driving much too fast for the transportation of a normal client. Fearing that it was indeed Jukka in the back seat of the cab, in search of me, I leapt out of the jeep and looked around wildly. For lack of a better idea, I crept under the small overpass bridge at the end of the street, happy that the drizzle had turned into an angry torrent and might keep anyone from spying me.

It was a low-slung bridge, and I had to stoop to keep from hitting my head as I scaled the small incline of bare dirt beneath it. Dizziness caused by the excesses of the night before, as well as a sudden rush of fear, suddenly overcame me. The rain was coming down in sheets, and I doubted I could make it back to the jeep and attempt a belated getaway in my suddenly enervated state without falling.

Halfway up the bare-dirt incline under the bridge, there was a depression in the earth. It was almost the exact shape and size of a mummy's coffin, with what could have been the outline of a human head at the top and a swelling in the curve halfway down to accommodate the arms. Just like a preserved, bandaged corpse, I lay down inside it. Its curves fit almost perfectly around my prone body; and it was deep enough to shield me to some degree from the spray-laden wind, which came in gusts through the open spaces on either side and concealed me as well, I hoped, from any prying eyes.

From my position I could see the taxi screeching to a halt, narrowly missing back-ending the jeep. Through the sheets of rain, without lifting my head, I couldn't make out the person who jumped from the back of the cab, so I stayed pressed into the earth. However, from the sounds I next heard, I surmised that the cab was pulling away; and afterwards, someone seemed to be opening the door of the jeep. He (or she?) wouldn't be able to start it, of course; the keys were hidden safely in my pocket. But I supposed there was as good a chance as any that it could be Jukka, in pursuit.

Then I don't know what happened. The rain suddenly began to come down with such ferocity that all images and sounds beyond the underside of the bridge were cut off by it. With each gust of wind, sheets of it were flung at me under the bridge, and my body was bathed in its iciness. But for the first time, I blessed the rain, because I knew it was my only chance of remaining concealed. There even seemed to be something ritualistic about it, a strange, violent baptism toward which other experiences in this region had been leading.

As those in a panicked state of suspension are wont to do, I let my eyes move around in an attempt to distract myself from the eternity of these moments. If you thought about it, this really wasn't very different from the inside of a mummy's tomb. There were calligraphic scrawls on the walls that from this distance could have been thought of as cuneiform. Along the rear side, where the incline at its steepest met the bottom of the bridge, which I could see by straining my head backward with all my might, someone had left a trail of artificial flowers and leaves. One of the inscriptions was large enough to make out from my position. It said, "Thank you, Kurdt. All I knew I learned from you."

Who was "Kurdt"? And why did this place, punctuated by the continual hammering of rain and the hysterical gurgle of the river, with a view of broken pilings like stalactites in the water beyond, feel so sepulchral? I wrestled with the thought only for a few moments, before passing into unconsciousness.

When I awoke, no one had found me; it was completely dark, and the iciness had invaded my muscles and bones to such a degree that I could hardly move. Groaning, and with enormous effort, I managed to change to a sitting position, then roll out of the depression in the dirt. The rain had stopped, and I could see from under the bridge that the jeep was gone—towed away, I figured.

Stooping, I walked toward the walls to examine them more closely. Obviously, this entire place was some kind of makeshift shrine to somebody. Complicated, faded spirals of graffiti covered the pitted beams, coalescing into the circled A that was a symbol for anarchy. Names and salutations were scrawled across the ceiling, and a small memorial against one wall still held a half-burned candle and some dried wild flowers.

There were other legible messages, as well. One said, "Being here doesn't feel real, I never thought I'd be under this bridge, here where you were. I'll see you in a better place, maybe." Another sentence, in someone else's writing, contained only the cryptic message: "I Love Jesus Doesn't Want Me For A Sunbeam. It makes me feel really kewl and reminds me of a small town."

It was too dark to read any of the other inscriptions—they'd been reduced to phosphorescent spirals that glimmered in the dark. The waves of the adjoining river caught gleams from the streetlamps above the bridge and sent ghostly green rays coasting along the beams and pilings. The entire scene filled me with an inexplicable sadness, so I walked out and down the street.[81]

---

81. Fortiphton had stumbled upon the bridge under which Kurt Cobain, who spent his youth in Aberdeen, was said to have lived during a homeless period. The depression in the earth under the bridge is thought to have been dug by Cobain, to sleep in. All the messages scrawled on the walls under the bridge— including the one mentioning Nirvana's *Jesus Doesn't Want Me for a Sunbeam*—are penned by Cobain fans, who make pilgrimages to the place and consider it a shrine. Poor Fortiphton never even knew he'd napped in the body outline of the departed singer.

IX

A Home at the End of the World

"Another listless day."[82] Rain spattered the tarpaulin reminding me that something called the world exists, and I felt a silly grin spread over my face at the thought of the powerlessness of it—I mean the world—because the rain itself, of course, is inescapable. Friday was in one of his trances again... Oh, but I'm getting ahead of myself.

For a moment, as I penned those words, it didn't occur to me that no one could possibly know—where I am, I mean. Despite the fact that the search for me must have been quite relentless, at this point. It certainly would have had to have been, given the unexpected outcome of the simple plan they'd concocted. And how simple it was, I thought I realized: Research and snag one alienated writer, just emerged from a legal crisis. Lure him to a place guaranteed to exaggerate his isolation and alienation. Use information about his recent problems to tempt him with young flesh and aggravate his penchant for anarchy. Build on his confusion by exposing him to a handsome smuggler of illegal aliens. Then move in for the

---

82. From one of many bizarre emails sent by Fortiphton, whereabouts unknown: "Narcissa, I can't tell you where I am. But be so kind as to do me a favor and make sure that if my manuscript ever sees the light of day, you'll get my film references and quotes right." What follows are a list of quotations and references, some of which don't even appear in the text. However, they include: "'Another listless day.'—Eloise Crandall in her diary, from *Female on the Beach*, starring Joan Crawford, dir. Joseph Pevney, 1955."

kill and use coercion, if necessary, to draft him to the cause of gathering the young and disenfranchised into a plebeian army. Presto! He's part of a movement to plunge a region—already shot with the violence of untamed nature—into a state of Zerzanian primitivism.

But why me? Certainly my skills as a writer would have no purpose in their future pre-verbal utopia. Or was I later to be offed, like other reactionaries had been, in other revolutions. None of it made sense, possibly because all of it now hovered in another dimension, like a mental construction that had nothing to do with the cells of my body. In this current state of vertigo and swirling pleasure, which resembled an endless descent through a perfectly thrilling spiral, all I could do was put my head in my hands and struggle to put thoughts together, for you, the reader, as if I were still writing this travelogue. All I could do was decide that I'd go on with this account, because… because I still have a nagging penchant for coherence.

Where to pick up? With Jukka and his mesmerizing limbs of betrayal, his blue-gray eyes of tin; that minion of the treacherous Machu Stapler, who plotted to enlist me in a foul scheme? Or crawling from the bridge in darkness, staring at the empty space where the jeep had been, thinking that Jukka had to have recovered it with another key or with the help of a locksmith or tow truck? Or at the Portland airport, where I shook with fear at the thought that this was just the place my assailants might look, as I was informed by an agent in nauseating microfiber mauve that a ticket to New York whose price matched the amount of money left in my pocket would require a wait of a whole three weeks?

Then there is my fuddled flight by bus and ferry to Vancouver, to put as many miles between me and my assailants as possible, my figuring that after a week or two I'd find a way to fly back East…

Every whirling fragment seems insignificant to me now, as I try to piece together the events of the last weeks, crouched as I am in this tiny tent on Hastings and S. Abbot streets in Vancouver, my roof more water-tight than all the others. My friend Friday, you see, was trained by his people in the weaving of tight mats from the fibers of split spruce roots and cattails and has skillfully braided the ripped garbage bags we collected into a tarpaulin that is impervious to the most insistent rain.

I met Friday just down the street, at one of Vancouver's many social services offices, although I was soon to learn that all these offices do is subject us homeless to a dreary, self-righteous evaluation. Their talk is full of all kinds of good-intention rhetoric borrowed from the lingo of missionaries; after which—once evaluated for violence—you end up discharged but still penniless, with nothing but a speedy ride to the nearest Greyhound and a free ticket in your pocket linked to a cheerful suggestion to leave town.

And no, it isn't because they're heartless. It's just because Vancouver has the bad luck of being at the spout of the North American funnel of desperation. It's the only urban locale in Canada where the homeless are unlikely to freeze to death in winter, the season in which all converge upon "Canada's California," as they call it, a perfect destination for the roofless down-and-out. Not to mention that phenomenon that some of my fellow bums refer to as "the gook invasion," a massive real-estate grab that the city is still reeling from, by rich industrialists from Hong Kong, after the Chinese takeover of that city, pushing housing values to an all-time high and forcing thousands more of the indigent into the street.

We—Friday and I—were among these unlucky indigents, creeping away from the Greyhound station as soon as the social services car drove off, falling silently into step together to head up Powell Street for Oppenheimer Park, which is really nothing more than a rectangle of sparse grass, like a football field, ringed by an international, interracial circle of junkies, who spend all day injecting their favorite substance into their most workable vein, while a cheerful outreach worker bides his time making batches of powdered lemonade.[83] Behold, then, yet another strange phenomenon in this gateway to the vast northern nowhere; it's the final destination of the West Coast drug runs, beginning in the marijuana fields and cocaine factories of Mexico and South America and poppy farms of the Far East.

But what was I doing in Oppenheimer Park? To be perfectly honest, I'll admit that my morphine supply had long ago been depleted; and other substances that I will not describe in detail slowly crept into place. This is what linked me with Friday, who claimed that a broken back and neck in a bus accident necessitated 1,000 mg of morphine a day, long ago denied by the merciless doctors but supplanted by the smokeable heroin in abundance here at "the Op."

Although our steps were in sync, I didn't notice him at first. I was much too enthralled by the tale of the young crackhead from Panama City who'd spent two months reaching this chemical Shangri La, a pilgrimage delayed when a hitchhiked ride in the back of a van took him to a suburb in New Mexico, where he was confined with others in a cellar, as part of a blackmail operation.

---

83. I'd laugh if I weren't beyond dismay at this point. We're taken on a visit to the skankiest park in a city that can boast one of the greatest on the continent: Stanley Park, a 1,000-acre wonderland of cedar flanked by beaches. I suppose we can forget about Fortiphton ever offering us any description of its miles of hiking and biking trails, its seawall boardwalk and multiple swimming pools.

The blackmailers would force those imprisoned to call relatives (they had a cheap international calling plan) and beg money for their "bail." However, the intrepid Panamanian escaped when the ceiling above his cellar exploded (they were also running a speed lab), and he scrambled out a window shattered by the shock, lacerating himself enough to be picked up in a downtown store by an ambulance, which took him to the hospital, from which he fled to continue his hitchhiking to this Promised Land.

At that juncture of the story, I suddenly blanched, stricken again by fearful ideas that have taken on the guise of hallucinations. I thought, Oh no, could he, could he possibly, be part of that vast reserve of disenfranchised youth whom Machu Stapler... and I turned away from him quickly.

That must have been the moment that I noticed the liquid brown eyes of the oft-silent Friday. Well... his name actually isn't Friday, of course. Friday is no name for a member of the Quileute Indian tribe of the Pacific Washington coast, whose past as whale harpooners and seal clubbers may be lost but isn't forgotten. He was part of the substantial Native American population of the city, referred to by the locals simply as "natives." His name was just a racist moniker on my part, because on this new island, bereft of every possession and stripped of every previous conception, I'd decided to construct a new reality, step by step and item by item, in the manner of that famous hero invented by Defoe. And into my *solitude curieuse* stepped this island assistant and guide.

When each of us had been sated with our substances, it seemed natural for Friday and I to stroll back together down Powell Street, recounting our respective biographies and combining our twin ingenuities into a plan for shelter. I told Friday that I was in hiding from some very evil men, who'd masqueraded as purveyors of educational information but were really organizing a dangerous revolt. And then I launched into each station of my itinerary, explaining how all of it had been designed to lead to a climax in Port Angeles, which would involve me in the Fagan-like enlistment of desperate young vagrants, for the sole purpose of plunging our social order into that same turbulent chaos that now raged in the natural phenomena of the region: a campaign of vandalism as ferocious as the gale that strips the tree of every leaf; and arson that chars like bolts of lightning; and finally, social upheaval like a great wave, powerful enough to send the severed trunks of our politics and culture smashing against one another, as they do in the ocean up here. Then I told how their plan, to my great delight, had been thwarted by my escape; and how I could thus enjoy my position as one of the saviors of our law and order.

Whether one is homeless or not, this is a mercilessly exposed city, with its surprisingly long shadows at noon caused by its northern location; its harsh, aluminum sunlight and sudden polar caresses; its endless boulevards of raw lifestyle: pawn shops, flophouses and head shops. Trapped between sea and mountains in the far southwest corner of British Columbia, it's like an open maw, framing the infinite distances of nature, gobbling up the helpless and regurgitating them into a terminal void.

Snow-capped mountains loom unexpectedly from the northern vistas. Its fingerlike peninsulas tremble from a chill among its many Pacific inlets; and as it stretches north, its outer reaches dwindle into wilderness, necessitating the hiring of bear patrols on suburban streets. Beyond this last stop of the empire is nothing but sea or polar region; and for many coming all the way from Toronto or El Salvador, it's the ultimate end of the line.

As Friday and I marched along this esplanade-into-emptiness of a city, his less spectacular story leaked meekly from him; reasonable as it sounded, I suspected it was a lie. He portrayed himself as a skilled, intrepid bus driver, who shepherded crowds across the Canadian boundary to the U.S. and back, but whose career was ended cruelly by a gargantuan collision, from which every passenger emerged unscathed save he, who broke both back and neck, entailing months in a cast in league with Morpheus and a future of chronic pain and bed-wetting.

The latter, at least, was true, as I was soon to experience, because we were destined to be roommates. Past the hemp stores and head shops and sprawling Bowery-like saloons, we discovered a former department store at Hastings and Powell that had been occupied by those in the same pickle as ourselves. We were quick to choose what used to be the perfume counter as our little corner of this makeshift longhouse,[84] but such domesticity endured barely a week. It seems that the liberal but centrist city fathers had suddenly approved the conversion of the building into posh apartments; and just as we were getting used to squatting inside, we were violently flushed out. So we moved into outer quarters with hundreds of others, in tents around the periphery, fully aware that another confrontation with the police was inevitable and that this time it would undoubtedly become very violent.

It was on that first night outside, under our expertly woven garbage-bag tarpaulin, that Friday verified his bed-wetting tendencies. But I didn't mind, because by that point I was already mesmerized by the net of mythological safety he'd woven around

---

84. A long communal dwelling used by some North American Native Americans.

me. He recounted the creations of the Great Transformer, who had reached his land on the Washington coast and seen only two wolves and no humans. Transforming the wolves into people, he told them, "Because you come from wolves, you shall be strong and brave in every manner." For this reason, ferocious Friday had not the slightest fear of our coming confrontation with the cops because, as he explained, he had the heart and cunning of a wolf.

Friday also soothed me with merry tales of a prankster known as the Raven,[85] who had put the sun in the sky and salmon in the rivers. Raven could assume any physical form at all, Friday would explain, holding his glass pipe over a piece of aluminum foil that held his customary sticky brown powder, which he heated with a match that he held under the foil. And after those words, as he exhaled the thin white smoke into the chill air, his eyes would lapse into a cunning, teasing smile, as if he were hinting that he himself might be that legendary character. He did look otherworldly. His mostly pleasant, tan, round face was, in fact, flattened in a strangely smashed way; but he attributed this to being of noble birth.[86]

---

85. The most important mythological character of the Pacific Northwest indigenous people, sometimes appearing as the Transformer himself and sometimes taking the guise of a trickster. It has led me to reconsider footnote 76 in which I identified "raven" as a male prostitute working in collusion with espionage agents.

86. I'd be more inclined to "attribute" it to Friday's bus accident. The practice of flattening the foreheads of noble Quileute infants by tying them to the cradle board—in order to signify beauty and rank—has been "out of style" for some decades.

He could stare into space for hours on end in some kind of meditation, a practice that trickled onto me, creating a kind of bliss. When food was scarce, he eased the growling in my stomach by saying that we were preparing for a spirit quest that required ritual cleansing. Then he'd lapse back into his wordless trance, staring at a tiny braid in the tarpaulin.

Friday's word phobias often caused me to use circuitous language. There were words that I wasn't allowed to use in his presence because they referenced the names of deceased relatives, and these names were forbidden to be spoken for a period of ten years.[87] I once made a quip about my body hair, in comparison to his, which was totally absent. Friday blanched and placed an index finger to his lips, because his deceased dad, Harry, a chronic alcoholic, had succumbed to 43 years of the substance in 1994. He cautioned me to call the trousers I wore dungarees, and not jeans, since his mother, who'd slipped in the shower and cracked her skull two years ago, had been called "Genie." Dollars and coins weren't taboo, but "bills" were, recalling Friday's unfortunate bro' William, who'd caught HIV from needles, diminished to a walking skeleton and finally done himself in by shooting a speedball.

If there was one of Friday's peccadilloes that annoyed me, it was his obsession for lady's underwear.[88] Dressed every day in a death-rocker black leather jacket, olive army pants and boots,

87. Bizarre that Fortiphton's references actually are in accordance with known Pacific coast Native American rituals, or would be if this were happening more than eighty years ago. The Quileutes once had numerous taboos about corpses and the dead, including a taboo about mentioning the names of deceased relatives.
88. Certainly no Quileute nor any other Native American custom!

he'd go so far as to give up a daily dose for a new pair of the frillies, which he enjoyed stroking and sometimes even wearing under his ultra-macho garb. Because they were frequently soiled by his nocturnal bladder problems, we spent the better part of several days a week replenishing the supply, usually lifting them from The Bay, a department store on Granville and Georgia. But when things got hot there, we had to move our operations to some boutique shops on Robson Street. It was a small price to pay for his friendship, because I learned so much from him.

Browsing Vancouver's many Goth shops, with their displays of skull-encrusted crosses, heavy-metal tee-shirts and temporary stick-on tattoos, or strolling through adjoining Native American souvenir stores with their kitsch soap-stone carvings, abalone-shell jewelry and hunting knives, we'd fall into long conversations in which Friday would indulge my obsessive fears about the subversive powers of this region. He'd listen peaceably and quietly to my stormy theories of disjunction,[89] a term I thought characterized these lands—their hodgepodge of suburban settlements, swaths of wild nature or decimated forest; and he seemed to understand my fear of having chanced upon something that was the opposite of civilization, a place in which "no specific system of order was proposed or desired."[90] Here were savage lands grabbed at random and without forethought, and never completely, by a changing roster of groups, all of whom believed in their hegemony but none of whom had ever brought the turbulence under control.

---

89. A theory Fortiphton borrowed from (but didn't bother to credit to!) the sociologist and anthropologist Zhang Er.

90. Zhang Er, again.

"This is because no man is master of The Land," Friday would whimper in our tent, usually after he retold the story of how the Transformer made the tail of the beaver and after he'd asked me to inflict the same "punishment" upon him.[91] And when I'd obliged him and we lay side by side panting from the effort, with the patter of raindrops on our little roof and the feeling of being the only humans in some vast wilderness, Friday would explain my mistake in seeing myself in opposition to the turmoil that had so frightened me. "You can't oppose the land," he'd say. "You can only declare yourself a son of it."

As proof of this, he exhibited a surprisingly learned grasp of Vancouver's history, showing how the land at the basis of it had returned it to its natural equilibrium again and again. He would expound, quite often, at our favorite "wild west" bar, an establishment beneath the Hotel Dufferin, crawling with addicted rentboys, some of whom had concocted the most eccentric naked dances for the patrons, as a way of bringing in a few *sous*. When we weren't sitting in the Plexiglas-enclosed smoking area, where the air was thicker than a pea-soup London fog, we'd lounge before the small stage watching these erotic street craftsman, one of whom began his dance wearing an elephant-head mask and ended it tossing clouds of farina into the air.

It was during such cryptic moments that Friday would try to place Vancouver within a larger context, describing the anti-German riots that filled its streets during World War II and consumed German businesses in a furious conflagration; or the

---

91. Fortiphton is referring to the Quileute legend explaining how the beaver got its tail—that it was a humiliating punishment inflicted upon the animal by the Transformer who decreed that a paddle be inserted into its anal region.

government removal of Japanese Canadians from their fishing boats, after which they were shipped inland to camps in British Columbia and the Prairie provinces. He'd talk about the closing of the British Columbia border to non-white immigration in the 1920s or recount the 1886 fire that destroyed the city in a matter of minutes, less than a year after it had been christened. And then he would gesture almost grandly around us, at the smoke-filled Plexiglas cube or a naked boy miming the most obscene of the yogic positions onstage and say, "And these too are children of the Great Transformer, who destroys and builds in eternal cycles. The riots of the labor unions in 1910 and their confrontation with the soldiers, the white mob violence in Little Tokyo, the reduction of my people's land to a smidgen of its previous expanse are born from this and end in this, which is eternal. They are only a single heaving of Her (Friday was strangely politically correct) breath."

On those nights that Friday suffered insomnia, remembering some misbehavior as a child after which his parents had warned him that he would be kidnapped by the "daskiya,"[92] we'd sit up, huddled together, chatting. Gradually he would suggest that perhaps I'd gotten things wrong. Maybe my tormentors were actually teachers, he would surmise; to the student, the master sometimes appears in a threatening or even grotesque guise. Could they have sent me, he wanted to know, on a spiritual journey? Was this great upheaval I thought they were planning perhaps nothing more than a transformation of my erroneous preconceptions?

---

92. A mythical Quileute creature with hair made of kelp, said to carry off misbehaving children.

At first Friday's insinuations angered me; I even began to suspect he was a plant. Still, he persisted; until very gradually, they began to make sense on some level. Could this terrible cleavage between man and the natural world be nothing more than an ideological cleavage in me? Were nature and man on opposite ends of a dichotomy, or merely different aspects of an endlessly transforming single process? I'd mull this over, sitting alone in one of the mammoth taverns near Hastings, while Friday went in search of a five-dollar oral moment from one of the crack hookers who frequented the alleys near our home, or later that night, when he'd removed his lingerie and we'd just played punish-the-beaver-with-the-paddle.

"There is carnality in spirituality," he told me one night, after a particularly strenuous session. "Without a balance of them, you're flawed. They're like Heaven and Hell, but they must be united in the same person."

It was around this time that I woke up one morning in our tent and through the crack of space between it and the ground saw booted feet and khaki green pant legs walking by, which suddenly brought to mind that unforgettable image of Jukka standing between me and the light, an epic and unyielding silhouette, like a piece of Fascist sculpture. Indeed, there was something about the rhythm of the walk that made me think it really was he. Turning pale with fear was only half the reaction I had to the hunch; another part of me was consumed with a strange and inexplicable excitement. Friday, who'd zoned out to the sound of the wolf chants he played on the portable CD player we'd salvaged, immediately noticed the pallor in my face. And there we sat, with me rooted in sudden fear and longing and Friday silently studying my face.

That night, he asked to see the itinerary, which I'd carried since my flight in my pocket on a frayed and crumpled piece of paper—as if it were a talisman that couldn't be looked at but also couldn't be disposed of. I resisted vehemently, seized by the preposterous fear that unfolding the scrap would catch me in its web again. But finally, under the influence of Friday's mild, doe-like eyes, I removed it from my pocket and handed it to him.

He studied it for a moment and gasped. It was just as he'd expected, he exclaimed, holding the scrap under my nose and pointing out the last stop of the itinerary with a dirt-encrusted index finger. It said, "La Push."

"This is the place of my people," he explained, for although I'd heard much about his culture, he had never named the place from which he'd come. "Don't you see that you must go there?"

"They'll find me," I hissed with panic.

"This could be good," he daringly but cryptically mused.

There was little time to discuss the controversial proposition because suddenly a Billy club was smashing our tent. The strong weave held up to the assault, and I could hear the officer swearing. As soon as I saw the tear-gas canister poking in from the crack at the bottom, I scrambled to a sitting position and somersaulted out—into chaos. Plastic bags and nylon tents were floating in the air all the way up the block, like gargantuan confetti; and half-dressed or even naked people, some on their hands and knees, were milling dazedly about, snatching at their few possessions, as a helmeted riot squad dove through the mayhem like an angry torpedo and bullhorns blared commands to clear out.

Friday had disappeared as if he'd never existed. Perhaps in the shock of the situation, I hadn't even seen him run away. Coughing and gasping, with watery eyes, I ignored the rain of blows on my back to rummage through our now collapsed tent for my jacket and then my pants and—finally—this manuscript, water-stained and half handwritten. Clutching them to my chest, I dove into an alley and—standing on one leg—struggled into my pants.

X

Cloudcuckooland [93]

Black-feathered Night laid a wind-egg, which with the help of Eros and some golden pinions gave birth to the world. Eons later, humans defamed and enslaved these heavenly, winged creatures, the birds, even daring to feast upon their once-regal flesh.

Thus recounts Aristophanes in the quirky comedy *The Birds*, in which flying animals are organized to form an embargo, an aerial blockade covering the heavens with bright, soaring avian bodies, to keep sacrifices from reaching Zeus and other human gods in order to starve them into submission. In shrill notes, the birds sing our swan song, with the intent of destroying our pre-eminence and founding a new utopia. More than two millennia later, Alfred Hitchcock reprised nearly the identical theme. [94]

The situation had arose a third time on the angry shores of La Push as I watched the black birds wheel through the spray-laden air in flocks as dense as flying carpets. Then they would cluster on the small offshore islands like scabs and shriek their triumphant fury toward the heavens. It seemed astounding that their cries could out-shout the crashing waves, but they traveled over them, assaulting my ears in a fiendish-sounding chorus.

---

93. Fortunately, I minored in classics when I was a girl at U. Dub. This is a reference to the mythical bird city in Aristophanes' play *The Birds*.

94. *The Birds*, 1963.

Once out of Vancouver, getting here had been easier than I thought. A van of neo-hippies, laden with marijuana, picked me up on the highway not far from the city and took me with their car onto the ferry and over the border, even pooling their money for my ferry ticket. I sang for my supper by entertaining them with rollicking tales of my own hippy youth in the Bay area and stuck with them a hundred miles down the Washington coast. Then came a night ride farther south on US 101 from a lonely, grizzled truck driver, who had enough heart to slip me twenty for a few moments of oral pleasure. I found not the slightest rancor in his voice when he observed, "Aren't you getting a little old for this?" He let me off right at the divide of the Bogachiel and Sol Duc Rivers, and I walked the 17 miles south on highway 110, where I came upon this sea resort operated by the Quileute, right at the unruly mouth of the Quillayute River. Only because it was off season, the tribal clerk let me have a camper cabin without a toilet for the $20.

Exhausted but driven, I stayed inside less than a half hour to dry off from the drizzle. I kept hearing the raging sea through the walls of the cabin, like the great sucking sound that occurs as water rich with krill and plankton flows through the gaping jaws of a whale. It aspirated me outside to the beach as if I were the tiny, will-less prey of that great devourer. Here I saw the ballet of the amputated tree trucks—enormous logs that had been swept to sea by current or storm, smashing against each other in helpless agony. Here, as well, all my preoccupations were dwarfed to insubstantiality. No social upheaval could possibly match the one that now erupted before my eyes; and I remembered Friday's words, which had sought to restore the chaos within me to the natural.

I thought about the dog-eared manuscript lying inside the cabin, the cocky urban irony and contempt of its first several chapters, and how insignificant such observations and opinions seemed juxtaposed against this crashing panorama. Here there was no need for sly irony, which shriveled in the face of blatant, delirious conflict. The inconsequentiality of irony, then, was proof of the inconsequentiality of the individual. How much did only one shrieking, protesting bird matter? Woven together like the twistings of Friday's tarpaulin, however, they formed great, sweeping gestures of fatality.

That was when I chose to hike to town one more time and find a post office for my manuscript—until I realized I didn't have a cent remaining for postage. I prevailed upon the good will of the tribal clerk to mail it for me. Reading desperate urgency in my eyes, he wordlessly took it from my hands.

Like the speck of a far-off bird, I was diminished to the dot of nothingness we all are; and stepping over the enormous tree trunks that littered the shore, I moved in the rain toward the icy waves. Standing on a rock, I paused before my plunge, wondering what reason there was to stop me from becoming part of the great diffusion. There was nothing to keep me from sinking into the waves. They would carry me back to the primordial supremacy of the birds and lift me in that great dissolution that represents the final exit.

Just as I was bending at the knee for a leap into freedom, something touched me lightly on the shoulder. It was Jukka, but not the Jukka whose image I'd kept—and perhaps secretly cherished—in my mind. No, this was a cute, if rather bullish-looking, Northwestern youth, with mild blue eyes and a vigorous, eager mouth; and he looked, to my amazement, no different than dozens of young middle-class hikers, campers or students I'd seen in my travels here. He was nothing but a less handsome version of the pedestrian young Mercury I'd seen at the gallery show of Soft Architecture at the University of Washington.

For a moment my body convulsed in shock and fear at the thought that I must be the butt of some diabolical joke: a normal, wholesome suburbanite had been drafted to impersonate my sinister, militaristic bar pilot. Yet as soon as he spoke, I recognized the voice and knew it really was he. By some inexplicable twist, the soldier of fortune of my night terrors had become a pleasant-looking, laid-back Northwesterner.

"It's me, Johnny."

"Jukka?"

He broke into an embarrassed, though flattered grin. "Hey, nobody calls me by my Finnish name. You must have been doing quite some research. I've been here almost ten days, you know. You really had us worried. But Machu had a hunch you'd show up here sooner or later since it was the last stop of the trip. What the hell happened to you?"

I stared at him, pretending—God knows for whom—to be dumbfounded; but actually, I was having just the opposite reaction; I was feeling overwhelmed by clarity, invaded by a sudden calm, as if a veil had been lifted and my entire story had been pulverized into senseless, unrelated atoms.

"Come on," said Jukka. "Stapler's pal—the blond guy who works with him?—is waiting in the car over there. He came out a couple days ago, too. You know, you don't look so well. We're gonna take you back to Stapler's and then get you back to New York, Mr. Fortiphton."[95]

95. After the problems we've suffered from this felon's mischief! He barely warrants kid gloves. It seems to me that the patience of Stapler's outfit is uncalled for and verges on the saintly.

"OK, OK," I nodded with exaggerated politeness, like a nervous geisha. "Just let me get my stuff, I'll meet you at the car."

I watched Jukka—I mean Johnny—walk away from the beach toward the car, in all his quotidian corporeality, carefully wedging each of his steps between the boulders and logs; and then the strangest thing happened: suddenly the clouds parted, and a glorious sun pierced the sky. Cleaving the fog, it brought the tiny, stunted islands, covered with twisted green trees, into sharp focus. The rain stopped as if turned off abruptly by a faucet. Everything burst forth in sharp-edged Technicolor: pebbles, trees, islands and birds; and the sun, the sun, which plunged me into a bright, overwhelming reverie.

So I didn't return to my cabin. I made my way farther along the shore and fixed my eyes on a single, cawing black bird; it was just an angry speck, as inconsequential as me, dwarfed by the slimy giant log upon which it perched. But as I gazed into the sea, I saw that even larger logs were nothing in the hands of the heaving waves that batted them about like ping pong balls.

I stooped toward the waves and cupped a part of them in my hand, whereupon the substance of the waves, too, became clear nothing, and the waves lost their power and even their form.

Matter itself, the building block of nature, had instantaneously become insubstantial. Nature herself was nothing and ultimately formless, shimmering. All that really existed was this force, which at that moment I identified as the wind, howling in the shell of my ear like an eternal, unmodulated drone; and over it, or through it, penetrated Johnny's perky voice, sounding amiable but a little punctilious: "Mr. Fortiphton, come on, it's time to go, don't you know we've all been waiting for you!"

Walt Curtis
8426 Holcomb Boulevard
Oregon City, Oregon 97045

Howdy, Mach,

Woah! That Applegate lady sent me the manuscript you're thinking of publishing. Do me a favor, will you, and tell her not to call me again? It's just the voice, man, it's so goddamn piercing!

Anyway, I just want to tell you that I hardly know this Fortiphton dude. Yeah, we had a few beers when he came out west a couple times, and I thought he was a hoot. But that manure he was shoveling out about me? Whew! He sure has an overactive imagination. I only wish my life was that exciting!

My friend, Larry—have you ever met him?—he used to be a lawyer but got disbarred for stalking some chick—told me to cover my ass by writing you a letter and denying everything. So here it is:

I, Walt Curtis, deny everything.

Still, I got to say that the book's got a few laughs. Broad and obvious as they are. But you know those dogs of New York, they tend to chew up the scenery. He doesn't know shit about the history of this region.

Good luck with it, anyway.

Your friend,

Walt Curtis
The Peckerneck Poet

P.S. I'm thinking of putting together a volume of poetry about those couple of times I hung out with Fortiphton. "Futzing Around with Fortiphton" is the working title. What do you think? Would Clear-Mind be into it?

Narcissa Whitman Applegate
111 Hilldale Ave.
Beaverton, Oregon 97007

December 7

Dear Machu,

It's with great regret that I write this letter, but after four unreturned calls to your home, I'm contacting you this way as a last resort. As you know, Machu, I was delighted when you first offered me the chance to collaborate in the publication of a new travelogue on our area. Outsiders have yet to grasp the pleasure and privilege of living in a region whose natural and cultural richness outflanks, in my opinion, almost that of anywhere else in the country.

I suppose a lot of this is my fault. I should have alerted you about whom we were dealing with as soon as I chanced upon that information about Fortiphton's criminal background. But being of liberal mind, I felt the ethical duty to give him the same chances afforded all Americans.

Well, as I'm sure you agree, my good intentions have backfired. Instead of giving us an original—even quirky—book that will boost this area's status on the cultural map, he's thrown at us a compendium of perversity and viciousness, sorely lacking in any practical information, full of distortions, sarcasm—and even obscenities!

Of course, I assumed that you and I would be in agreement concerning this particular manuscript; and, believe you me, I tried to the best of my ability to point out in my annotations the warped misinformation I discovered, just in case you hadn't noticed all of it. But having heard that you actually still intend to publish this lunatic's text... My God, Machu... Now I've got the sad and unexpected duty of putting my foot down.

I know you as a valuable contributor to this community and a firm upholder of everything we believe in. How can you possibly think that the publication of these ravings will do anyone any good?

I implore you to think more carefully about the repercussions for both of us—not to mention your fledging company. If such considerations aren't enough to change your mind, consider the several insults to me in this text and the grotesque, absolutely false fantasies he's projected upon us both. To me they seem perfect fodder for a legal suit, I'm sorry to say. And I'd hate to go that far, Machu, and ruin our very cordial relationship. Please, don't force me to.

Yours,

Narcissa

ABOUT THE AUTHOR

Novelist, translator and essayist Bruce Benderson is the author of the memoir *The Romanian: Story of an Obsession* (2006), winner of France's prestigious Prix de Flore in French translation. He is the translator of *Good Sex Illustrated* (2007) by Tony Duvert for Semiotext(e).